"You could pass now for a boy,"

Wade drawled, his eyes flicking to her hair. "Did you cut it yourself, or were you training to take vows?"

"Don't be funny," she rejoined. "One of the sisters cut it for me. I worked at the mission, Major. I even scrubbed floors."

"Bravo for you. Something to tell the magazine editors when you get home. 'Debutante gets down on her knees to scrub and pray!'"

As he turned and entered the jungle, Eve followed him, hating his cynical sense of humor. High above her head a bird seemed to sing, "I was a good little girl...I was a good little girl...."

It sounded like the opening bars of a music-hall song, and Eve found herself finishing the line in her head...*till I met you!*

Books by Violet Winspear

HARLEQUIN PRESENTS

HARLEQUIN ROMANCES

These books may be available at your local bookseller.

For a free catalog listing all titles currently available, send your name and address to:

Harlequin Reader Service
P.O. Box 52040, Phoenix, AZ 85072-2040
Canadian address: P.O. Box 2800, Postal Station A,
5170 Yonge St., Willowdale, Ont. M2N 5T5

VIOLET WINSPEAR

time of the temptress

Harlequin Books

TORONTO • NEW YORK • LONDON
AMSTERDAM • PARIS • SYDNEY • HAMBURG
STOCKHOLM • ATHENS • TOKYO • MILAN

Harlequin Presents first edition March 1978
ISBN 0-373-10230-5

Second printing May 1980
Third printing June 1982
Fourth printing August 1982
Fifth printing October 1982
Sixth printing January 1983
Seventh printing November 1983
Eighth printing February 1984

Original hardcover edition published in 1977
by Mills & Boon Limited

Printed in U.S.A.

CHAPTER ONE

THERE was no doubt about it, the five nurses rescued from the mission must have seats on the aircraft. They were utterly exhausted and the older ones couldn't travel on foot another ten yards, let alone thirty miles through jungle to the coast town of Tanga, still free of rebel occupation ... so the pilot of the plane informed the man in khaki who had brought the nursing nuns this far to safety.

'The trouble is——' The pilot hesitated, and the dark, unshaven face of the soldier assumed a sardonic expression.

'Yes?'

Hearing the way he said it Eve Tarrant decided that he could put more meaning into a single word than anyone else she had ever encountered.

'As you can see, Major, the plane is loaded with folk already—if I overloaded I'd be risking a lot of lives for the sake of a few.'

'You must take the Sisters!' The words had the cutting edge of a jungle knife. 'They've had a grim time of it and you can see for yourself that they're on the point of collapse.'

The pilot swept his eyes over the nuns, still in their torn and grubby nursing habits, their faces drawn. His eyes settled on Eve, the youngest of them.

'I might manage the older ones,' he said, 'if some of my passengers agree to discard their baggage. But——'

'You take them all!' The words were explicit, the tough jaw was set; the soldier had no intention of being balked.

The pilot ran a troubled hand through his hair and half turned towards the plane as one of the passengers came to the exit.

'We should be on our way,' the man called out pompously. 'Every second we waste here, arguing, our lives are endangered.'

The tall lean soldier, with a shotgun slung on his shoulder by a strap, swept his eyes over the stout passenger in clean white drill. 'We can all see how anxious you are,' he drawled, 'but I must insist that these Sisters come on board.'

'But we haven't the room—our pilot has just said so!'

'Please'—Eve caught on impulse at the khaki-clad arm, 'if room can be found for Sister Mercy and the others, then I am sure I can trek the rest of the way.'

He looked down at her and his face was a leathery mask in which a pair of steel-grey eyes glittered. 'It's noble of you to offer, nurse, but I'm not noble enough to take you on. Our pilot friend is going to find room for all of you, even if I have to unload the stout one and all his nicely starched shirts and ducks in their leather cases.'

The man heard him and went turkey-red. 'I've paid for my seat, you darned mercenary!' he blustered.

The steely eyes raked the overfed face. 'Sooner that than a bloated clerk who sits on his rump while women and girls do the grim work out here and nearly lose their lives in the process. I think,' the rifle was significantly raised, 'we can make room for them by getting shot of you.'

6

'Steady on,' the pilot whispered fiercely. 'He's some sort of an official and I'm duty bound to get him to safety with some important documents he's carrying. I'll see if some of the passengers will allow their baggage to be left behind. That will lighten our load.'

Eve retreated to the shade of a flame tree on the edge of the forest clearing, and in a sort of tired dream she listened to the voices—like a distant surf—and heard the arguments regarding the baggage. She wanted poor Sister Mercy and the others to take off in the plane; they had endured two years of trouble and dangerous strife, whereas she had only been at the mission a couple of months. She was younger, not so worn out by tension as they. And still she wanted to prove to herself that she was more than a social butterfly, deb of the season, darling of the fashionable resorts, and good for nothing except a decorative life and a society marriage.

She had fled from all that, to help out, unpaid, at the mission. She hadn't dreamed that jungle revolt could be so frightening ... they had hidden in the cellars for days, with barely enough to eat and drink, until the mercenary Major had stormed in and forced them to come this far. There was something tough and unholy about the man ... he had known that if they could reach here by daybreak there would be a plane ready to take off to safety.

Suddenly his tall shadow fell over her and she glanced up at him, the tangled hair falling across her topaz eyes.

'Could you really trek it?' His voice was as hard as his sunburned features. 'I shouldn't relish having to carry you if you wrench one of those patrician ankles.'

Eve swallowed the retort that sprang all too readily

7

to her lips ... she had to remember that he had saved the lives of the nuns. 'Have you managed to find room for those poor tired women?'

'Just about. It seems there isn't a man on board who will gallantly give up his seat for a darling debutante.'

'Stop it—please!' Anger and weariness met in her eyes and they shimmered as if she might cry.

'Right.' He swung away from her and called out to the pilot: 'Take off now! Don't waste any more time getting those precious people to a hotel for tiffin on the veranda!'

The pilot inclined his head, set his jaw, and saluted the two who must stay behind to face the hazards of the jungle and the rebels. He climbed into the cockpit of his machine and as the engine throbbed, faces were pressed to the windows and Eve met the tired and defeated gaze of Sister Mercy. Then the good Sister glanced at the mercenary and she seemed to be saying: 'Trust him, child, though he looks in league with the devil himself.'

The plane took off, leaving in its wake a curious stillness, and a huddle of suitcases on the grass. Two were of expensive pigskin stamped with initials, one was circular and looked as if it had belonged to a woman, and another was battered with labels all over it.

'Well,' drawled Eve's companion, 'we shall with luck find you a change of clothing. You look as if you need it.'

'And so do you,' she retorted. Humour and a slight touch of hysteria joined forces inside her and suddenly she was laughing, leaning there against the tall tree hung with flamy flowers. 'You look like Humphrey Bogart in that film about Devil's Island!'

'We'll save the compliments for later, if you don't mind.' He gazed with a dark frown at the airfield bungalow, utterly deserted now that the last of the refugees had left. For days they had been arriving here and the planes had been flying in to pick them up, but there would be no more planes. This area was now evacuated, and Eve and the man whose name she did not know were the only human beings in the vicinity. The monkeys had drifted back to their treetop perches, and gaudy parrots sat together on a long branch and nagged one another. It was a strange, unreal moment, that breathless interval running and then coming to a halt, with danger held at bay by chance ... or by the assertive thrust of a masculine chin, and a hard brown hand holding a hunting rifle. Eve knew it wasn't a military weapon by the polished butt of reddish wood and the copper plate with a name inscribed. She had a vision of him snatching it from the wall of an abandoned plantation house, and handling it with the authority of a hunter.

She watched as, like a silent cat, his every nerve a coiled spring of alertness and daring, he mounted the steps of the airfield bungalow and thrust open the wire-meshed door. He stood there looking in, a tall individual, with his skin weathered to a shade of brown that made his eyes arresting, swift and glancing as a rapier tip. The strength of his jaw and the width of his shoulders gave him a formidable air. He made Eve feel hostile, because never had her existence held such a man, a soldier of fortune, who roamed where the rebellions were, and who rescued a weary group of women as if he were pulling kittens out of a stream into which a cruel hand had thrown them.

Several words to describe him sprang to her mind, and then the door swung shut and he was inside the bungalow and she knew him to be searching the rooms to make sure no enemy was hiding there. He left her feeling lonely, there in the compound with the jungle behind her, and suddenly she was running towards the steps and panic was at her heels.

'Major . . . !'

'I'm here.' He emerged from a doorway and regarded her with cool eyes. 'The place is quite deserted, but it has a kitchen and I hope it will yield some food. Are you hungry?'

She thought about it and realised that she was. In their flight appetite had been forgotten, but now she became aware of a gnawing pang at her midriff. 'I'm awfully hungry.'

'Then let's ransack the kitchen.'

'Dare we? Have we . . . time?'

'We must make time and hope for the best. The sound of the plane will have been heard, but for a while this place will be assumed to be deserted. Come along, the kitchen is at the end of this corridor.'

There in the dim recesses of a store cupboard they found a few tins containing coffee, corned beef, plum jam, and quite a hoard of beans. They scrambled together some of the beef and beans, heating them over the Primus stove, and made hot, strong coffee, none the less welcome for its lack of milk and sugar.

'Eat hearty,' Eve was urged. 'You're going to need, young deb, all the strength you can muster for the jungle trek ahead of us. Our thirty miles might turn into forty if we have to make any detours, or the going is particularly tough.'

10

'I—I wish you wouldn't call me "young deb" in that scornful voice.' Her cheeks stung. 'My name is Eve.'

'Is it really? Well, I don't answer to Adam or Humphrey.' His grin was so wicked it was satanic. 'I'm called Wade.'

'Wade?'

'Don't you care for the name?'

'I think it highly suitable, for someone who wades in where angels fear to tread. Do I call you Major Wade?'

'It's my christian name. The surname is O'Mara.' He spoke drily and began to pack the tins of food into his knapsack, not forgetting the opener. 'It's a pity we can't take the Primus, but it's a trifle too bulky for our trek. Come, let's take a look in the lounge. There may be something that will come in handy.'

'I suppose it's all part of your job,' she said, 'to ransack the places you come across?'

He gave her a silent, steady look out of those keen cool eyes, and her nerves felt agitated by a strange fear of him. She realised how alone she was with him. Sister Mercy and the huge silver cross that hung around her neck on a chain of tiny prayer beads was no longer there to protect a girl from this type of man. Eve summoned her most defiant look, and saw a slightly derisive smile quirk on his lips. He was equally aware of their isolation together ... the mercenary and the debutante!

'You've just reminded me that we have those suitcases to ... ransack. I'll fetch them and we can sort out what we need. I think you will agree, Eve, that we might as well take the best of the pickings before our rebellious friends arrive to tear everything apart and to make a bonfire of it all.'

A shiver ran through her and she hastened out with

11

him to the compound, and lugged back into the bungalow the circular case that one of the women passengers had allowed to be tossed from the plane. There in the lounge Wade forced open the case with a blade of the all-purpose knife he carried and they set to sorting through the contents. Eve found cosmetics, some sheer lingerie, a bottle of scent, a couple of illustrated magazines, and a pot of caviare!

She held it up for Wade's inspection. 'No champagne to go with it?' he drawled, and he tossed her a pair of slacks and a green silk shirt. 'I don't know what kind of a guy wore these togs, but I think I can guess. He was fairly slim anyway, and they should be all right for you. Here's a blazer as well ... catch!'

She caught the things and knew from the feel of them that they were expensive, probably brought out from England from a shop in Bond Street.

'Don't go too far away to change into them.' The order came in that explicit tone of voice, as if she were a trooper at his command.

'Aye, aye, sir. Will the kitchen do?'

'I'd prefer you to go behind that big leather couch. Time is speeding and I'd hate our friends to catch you with your pants down.'

'You might remember, Major, that I'm not one of your soldiers!'

'There isn't a moment when I don't regret that you aren't.' He glanced up from the more battered suitcase with the labels stuck all over it. 'Believe me, dear deb, I look forward to this trek as much as you do.'

'I'm not helpless, Major!' she retorted.

'Good at tennis and hockey, no doubt? First rate at a fancy skim round the dance floor or the ice rink? And a smash hit with the boys!'

'Oh . . .' Her fingers clenched the clothing which had belonged to the sort of young man she had been accustomed to. 'You really enjoy getting at me, don't you? Would you mind telling me why?'

'Because you're a social orchid from the tips of your ears to your tiny toes. The type who's at the root of much of the trouble out here—oh, you mean well, but you'd do better to stay at home adorning the fashion salons and the cocktail bars.'

Eve stared at him and went so pale that her eyes took on a denser shade of topaz. 'How can you lay the blame on me?'

'Your sort, little one. Born with a jewelled spoon between your lips, sweetly arrogant in your self-approval, and so sure that everything you do for the *lower orders* is a benefit rather than a bore.'

'Thank you very much!'

'You're welcome, Eve.' He gave her a sardonic bow, lean and every inch a fighter in his jungle uniform bearing the shoulder crowns of his rank in the mercenary army. 'Now, your ladyship, discard that uniform and change into the slacks and shirt, and splash yourself with this insect repellent.' He handed her the fat yellow tube. 'We're about to take a hike through country where the mosquitoes will just love that milky skin of yours, so be lavish with the cream and cover your limbs as much as possible—and do stop looking as if fate has landed you a wallop round the jaw. I may not be polite company, but I know the jungle and will do my utmost to get you to the Tanga coast.'

Grabbing a slip and panties from the circular case, Eve went behind the club couch and removed her torn and grubby uniform, which she soon replaced with the fresh underwear and the male outer garments. Because

13

she was tall the slacks weren't a bad fit, and she supposed that Wade O'Mara had selected the green shirt because to him she was such a greenhorn.

'Bring the uniform with you,' he ordered.

Eve did so and watched silently as he folded it among the garments they must leave behind. 'Show me your footwear,' he said, and when she extended a foot he looked rather grim. 'Our foppish friend has sandals in his case, but you have aristocratic feet! Come, try one of these.'

She obeyed, but the sandal felt like a boat. Suddenly she began to laugh and couldn't stop, and Wade gave her a rough shake. 'I'm going to cut some inner soles from the top of this leather case and it's going to waste precious time, but you must have a pair of decent walking shoes or I shall end up carrying you halfway home.'

'And neither of us would relish that,' she said, pleased that she could sound so definite about it. He gave her a brief look, a shimmer of silvery-grey, then he bent over his task, cutting deeply into the leather with his knife and hacking out a chunk of it. He then stood her worn-out shoes upon it and traced round them with the knife blade ... his hands were as brown as the leather and as tough, and yet they had a curious dexterity which produced in as short a time as possible a wearable pair of soles for the over-large sandals. He fitted them inside and told her to try the sandals once again. She did so and found them a lot more snug.

'Well, how do they feel?' he asked, snapping shut his knife and thrusting it into the sheath at his belt.

'Not too bad at all.' She swallowed her antagonism. 'Thank you.'

'Now is there anything in that woman's case that you'd like to take along ... and I don't mean the paint and the sheer wear.'

'A book might come in handy, also the comb and mirror ... do you know, Major, that pilot must have thrown off the wrong case. No woman would give up ...' Eve broke off and looked into the grey eyes. An eyebrow quirked above them and the firm mouth took a dent in it. 'You mean he did it on purpose? Because I'd need a few things?'

'Some men can be gallant. I never learned the trick of it.'

Sudden tears shimmered in her eyes and she bent closely over the case so that he wouldn't see that she was touched by the pilot's gesture ... lord help him when he landed his passengers!

'Can we take the little pot of caviare? It won't take up much room, and it's nourishing food.'

'Drop it in.' He held open his knapsack and she saw that he'd added the food cans, a shaving-gear from the leather case with the labels, a copy of a Penguin thriller, and one of those long silk scarves men wear with evening clothes. She couldn't think why he wanted it, unless he had a secret craving for the minor luxuries. Maybe that was why he was allowing her to have the caviare.

'Have you everything you want?' he asked.

'We might need a rug, and this plaid dressing gown might come in handy as a substitute. I can carry it, Major.'

'Okay, but don't overload yourself. The heat in the undergrowth will be near intolerable during the daylight hours. Now we'll stow these cases in a corner, as if they were abandoned there instead of outside, and we'll be on our way.'

'Have you remembered to fill your water bottle?'

Eve felt she had to ask, and to let him know that she was aware of the dangers and discomforts as he was, despite his opinion of her as a flimsy creature of flighty pursuits and efforts that were more of a hindrance than a help.

'Yes, the water bottle is full to the brim,' he replied, that droll note in his voice.

'I'll carry it——'

'No, you might lose it. All set?'

'Yes, Major.'

'And stay close to me, I don't want to lose you.'

'I rather thought it wouldn't worry you,' she mumbled.

'I beg your pardon?' He was busy guiding himself, his rifle and knapsack, now full, through the mesh door into the brilliant sunlight flooding across the compound. 'What did you say?'

'Nothing important.' She followed him and blinked against the sun, still strong and strange to her even after two months. The ceiling fans had still been purring in the bungalow, left on and forgotten by the staff who had left on the final plane. It had been cool in there, and now all at once she felt the impact of the tropical heat burning against her skin and hair. She would welcome their entrance into the jungle itself, where the trees would offer shelter from that burning sun, even if at the same time the green canopy closed in the warmth and made of the jungle a living greenhouse.

'Come, we must hurry,' Wade threw over his shoulder. 'We've wasted precious time enough ... are those sandals quite comfortable? I don't want you breaking an ankle.'

16

She followed him towards the trees, and though the sandals were still rather loose the thongs across the instep kept them from falling off, and it was rather like walking in house slippers. 'Yes, they're okay,' she said, falling unaware into his laconic figure of speech.

He reached the trees and turned to give her a sardonic glance, one that took her in from her feet to her titian hair. He was tall against the trees, the combat jacket straining against the wide bones of his shoulders. The rest of him was lean and long, topped off by a thatch of rough black hair. His very darkness had a danger to it, and the only light thing about him was the steely grey of his eyes.

Eve and he seemed in this moment to assess one another as hostile strangers about to be guests in a strange house; two people who must learn to accept each other's foibles for a short and intimate while. Colour ran beneath her skin and settled on the heights of her cheekbones, and the slight curves of her body hardly disturbed the green silk of the shirt she wore outside the band of the grey-green slacks.

'You could almost pass for a boy,' Wade drawled, and his eyes flicked her smooth cap of titian hair. 'Did you cut it yourself, or were you actually training to take vows?'

'Don't be funny,' she rejoined. 'One of the Sisters cut it for me so I'd feel cooler working about the mission. I really did work, Major. I even scrubbed floors.'

'Bravo for you. Something to tell the magazine editors when you get home. Should make quite a head-line: "Debutante gets down on her knees to scrub and pray!"' And so saying he turned and entered the jungle, and as Eve followed him, actively hating his cynical sense of humour, a bird seemed to sing high above her head: '*I was a good little girl . . . I was a good little girl . . .*'

It was odd, rather like the opening bars of an old music-hall song, and Eve found herself finishing the line in her head.

'*. . . till I met you!*'

CHAPTER TWO

A LOT of the country around the mission had been cleared for plantations and livestock, but Eve now found herself in the actual jungle, where wild snaking vines bound the trees together and laid traps for unwary feet, where ropes of convolvulus hung thick as an arm and loaded with the big bell flowers that smelled so primeval. Long, broad banana leaves had to be beaten out of their path, and whiplike bamboos had to be avoided. It was exhausting, the continual avoidance and beating back of jungle growth, all so alive, somehow, as if it would gobble them up. And the heat was cloying, so that Eve could feel the perspiration running down her skin and soaking the clothes that kept her from being badly bitten around the legs and arms. The mosquitoes seemed to lurk in the lower growth, among the enormous ferns and massive leaves around the boles of the trees. All was dim and green and seething with insect noises, broken by the crunch of Wade's boots, breaking down the path as much as possible so that she wouldn't stumble in her cumbersome sandals.

She dared not think of all the miles they must travel until they reaached the coast. She felt dismayed by the very thought of hours, perhaps days in this living greenhouse, where like a pair of human flies they battled with the giant foliage.

'What happens,' she asked suddenly, 'if the coast is in rebel hands?'

'We make for one of the villages. They're dotted about, and so off the beaten track that it's hard to believe there's a rebellion going on. Often the people are friendly and ready to help ... but my advice right now is don't waste energy thinking ahead, just keep walking and keep up your spirits.'

'I'm trying, but don't you have the feeling we're being watched all the time, every step we take?'

'Monkeys,' he said laconically, 'high in the trees. Curious about us but not dangerous.'

Eve smiled with relief, and wondered if there was anything on earth which could unnerve this Major of mercenaries, shatter the coolness with which he faced this journey and its hazards. Was he so hardened that nothing could make a dent in him?

He paused and his *panga* gleamed as he hacked a sprawl of lianas from their path. Now and again she had seen him consult a compass so she was free of the fear that they could become lost ... he might not be the most charming of travelling companions, but he was sure of himself, and a broad-shouldered bulwark against the menace that seemed to simmer behind her, and at every side of her.

She stumbled nervously when a parakeet screeched in the undergrowth, and at once he shot a look over his shoulder. 'Mind your step!' he ordered.

'I'm all right——'

'Would it help if I cut you a stick?'

'It might.'

'Then stay just where you are and I'll cut a bamboo.'

He disappeared into the denseness at the left of them, and Eve took a rest against the trunk of a huge old tree, shutting her mind to what its foliage might be hiding, and aware of a longing to slide down into the giant ferns and sleep. It seemed as if she had been on the move for hours, and indeed she had, for it had been some time last evening when the Major had searched the mission and found the Sisters and herself concealed in the cellar. All their patients had fled, or had been carried away by their families.

'We must keep going a while longer.' A bamboo stick cut at the joint was placed in her hand. 'This should make things a bit easier.'

'Thank you.' She looked defiantly into his eyes, as if to deny her weariness. He thought she lacked hardihood and she had to show him that she wouldn't be a burden on him. 'I know how imperative it is that we keep on going. and I shan't fall behind, Major, or make you wish too fiercely that I were a soldier instead of a stupid society girl who should have stayed at home in her cosy bandbox.'

He grinned in that brief and diabolical way of his. 'It will be something for you to remember, eh? Always supposing I get you to a boat or a plane.'

'I assure you this trek will be unforgettable!'

'And uncomfortable.' He faced about and they continued on their way, one behind the other, plodding tenaciously through an endless tunnel of green and shirring forest, brightened now and again by flame blossoms or a creamy curtain of wild orchids.

Eve thought of cool, faraway England. and the flaming quarrel she'd had with her guardian, who had been so sure that she would allow herself to become engaged to James Cecil Harringway the Third; heir to a corporation, good-natured and gangling, but not the man for Eve. She had stood out, and then on sheer impulse had packed a bag and flown to Tanga because she wished to help, to do something with the pampered life her guardian had made for her, only to expect in return that she marry a man she neither loved nor desired.

She plodded on in the wake of her guide, and felt sure that had her father not been killed when she was three, she would not be here in a steaming jungle, her face hot and shiny, and clad in the shirt and slacks of a man. Not only that, but at the mercy of a jungle mercenary, and a band of rebels who might be stealthily following their trail, or lying in wait for them at the coast.

Half an hour later they halted for a rest on a fallen tree, which Wade searched thoroughly for snakes before allowing her to sit down and relax. He handed her the water bottle and she took several grateful sips.

'More welcome than wine, eh?' He took his own few sips and then screwed the cap firmly into place again. 'Fancy a bit of chocolate?'

She shook her head and watched him enjoy some. He seemed quite untired, with an alertness in his eyes that made her think of a prowling animal that never slept or needed to. She felt curious about him and wondered if such a man had a wife, a family, a home in which he behaved like a human being. All she was certain of was his nerve, and that he had done startling and outrageous things. His only law was that of jungle lore!

'What conclusion have you come to?' he drawled.

'That I'm placed in the position of trusting a tiger.'

'The swift and silent brute who likes the shadows, eh?'

'The cat who kills for pleasure.'

He didn't reply and the jungle enclosed them as if in a green and echoing bell-glass. Eve wondered at her temerity in speaking as she had, but she didn't shrink away from him, or allow her eyes to waver from his face. He had been frank enough in his opinion of her!

'A million orchids,' he murmured. 'Back in England they cost the earth, and after an evening at the dance a girl preserves the orchid she has worn on her dress. So many of them must remind you of the times you've worn one to a concert or a ball?'

'I always preferred a rose,' she said quietly. 'Orchids have a clutching look about them.'

'They have no thorns.'

'True,' she said with a faint smile. So she had thorns, which meant she had pricked this man. She congratulated herself, and wriggled her toes in some ferns to cool them.

'You'll get bitten if you don't watch out,' he warned. 'Mosquito welts are not only irritable, they're painful and they can lead to a fever. I think when we make camp I'll dose you with a quinine tablet.'

'When do we make camp, Major?'

'When the sun goes down. The jungle will then be so dark as to be impenetrable, and I guess you need a night's sleep. We'll start at dawn tomorrow and make better time.'

'I hope I'm not too much of a hindrance,' she said, 'but I couldn't take a seat on that plane in preference to one of the Sisters. They had endured more than I ... oh, I don't want to sound self-righteous, but they were good to me. They understood why I came out here——'

'Were you running away from your life of luxury?'

'Yes, in a manner of speaking. You'd have been far more contemptuous of me had you known me before I worked at the mission.'

'Was there a young man involved?'

23

She shrugged and thought of James, who would be horrified, and startled, to see any girl less than immaculate. He was really one of those who believed that girls, like dolls, were kept in boxes in pretty dresses, with not a hair out of place. Girls like herself, who were brought up by nannies, who went to finishing schools, and drank champagne with their eggs and bacon.

'The silence of a woman always tells more than a torrent of words.'

Eve came out of her reverie as Wade spoke almost against her ear. She turned, startled, to look at him and found his eyes piercing hers and raking over the smooth, heated skin of her face, and taking in the features that had a Celtic purity to them. Her mother had been a Highland beauty, much painted by all the fashionable artists, and Eve was a true daughter of the isle of Arran, with eyes that reflected the misty lochs.

'So it was a man who sent you running out here to scrub and pray! Did you quarrel with him?'

'Yes,' she said, for it was all too true, and it wouldn't do any harm to let this mercenary Major believe that the quarrel had been with a man she loved. In a way it had been. She was fond of her rather arrogant guardian, and when she married she wanted to marry for love's sake. It was upon that issue they had flamed into heated words. 'I won't be sold in the marriage market,' she had stormed. 'I'd sooner work at Woolworths!' But as it happened she had read about the plight of Tanga in the newspapers, and being impulsive she had decided to be a heroine instead of a counterhand.

'Was he worth the predicament you now find yourself in?' Wade ran a hand down his unshaven jaw, and Eve winced at the rasp of the black bristles. The sound seemed to emphasise his maleness, and her total dependence upon his skill and his grit.

'I'm not sorry I came,' she said, meaning it. 'I've been of some use, even if you don't think so. I've seen suffering and courage, and I feel sure I'm a better person for knowing people such as Sister Mercy and the other nursing nuns.'

'Time will tell,' he drawled. 'When you find yourself in the Ritz Bar again, surrounded by admirers, you might soon forget the scent of ether and incense.'

'You're abominably cynical, Major!' She gave him a furious look. 'I can't imagine you believing in anything, except the chase and the kill.'

'Then your imagination will have to be attended to, young lady.' He rose to his feet, lean and supple as any tiger. 'Siesta is over, so rouse yourself, and get those toes back inside those sandals.'

Defiance flickered through her ... she wanted, as in the old days, to toss her Titian head and turn her back on a man. Her fingers clenched on the thick silk of the shirt he had commandeered for her, and she hated with her eyes that hard, fierce face of his. Heavens, how the tropics had browned his skin, burned his gentler feelings to a tinder, crinkled his eyes! Had he never danced to the last nostalgic waltz? Had wine never left its tears on the rim of a stemmed glass, while the petals drooped on flowers he had given a girl, and the candlelight died on the table?

'I know your feet are hurting and your spirits are wilting,' he said roughly, 'but this I have to do. On your feet, deb!' He enclosed her shoulder with his sunburned hand and forced her to rise. She wrenched free of him and struggled into the sandals with their leather soles as hard as his soul!

'Ready?'

'As I'll ever be, gallant Major!'

'Attagirl.' He gave a low, sardonic laugh, almost lost in the depths of his brown throat, and hoisting pack and rifle he stepped among the jungle trees, the webbing vines, the sticky spider nets, the primeval scents, and Eve followed him.

'I feel,' she said, 'as if I'm training to be a squaw!'

'Yes, you keep thinking along those lines and we'll get along fine, little one. Squaws are humble and obedient creatures.'

'Huh!'

'Did you stumble?'

'As if you'd care!' she snapped.

'I might take the trouble to give you a hand.'

'The back of it?'

Again he laughed, and a monkey leaped among the interlocking limbs of the trees and its tail seemed to whip at the trumpet flowers, showering petals like a mock confetti. A reluctant smile sprang to Eve's lips. It was good to see the monkeys, for their presence proved that she wasn't entirely alone with a human tiger.

For brief minutes she was amused, and almost secure, and then something dropped on to her and her scream tore the transient peace to shreds. She felt a wet stickiness all down one side of her shirt, and then Wade was beside her and she was giving him a dumb, stricken look.

'What the devil——?'

'W—what is it?' she gasped.

He touched her, and then gave a brief laugh. 'A bird's egg, probably tossed down on you by one of those mischievous monkeys. It's made something of a mess.'

'Ugh!'

'Better a broken egg on you than a palm rat, or a bird-eating spider. Stand still while I clean you up.'

She obeyed him, but couldn't quite control a contraction of her nerves as she felt him wiping her off with a khaki handkerchief large enough to cover a coffee tray. His hand brushed her body and she felt a sensation that actually frightened her more than the egg bursting against her. Their aloneness in the jungle was suddenly alive with alarming new meanings, and she was recalling some of the tales about mercenary soldiers which native girls at the mission had imparted to her.

Eve gave Wade O'Mara a quick fearful look, which he answered curtly in words. 'You can cut out what you're thinking.' He gave his handkerchief a shake. 'I don't go in for ravishing my hostages, not even a Titian-haired deb who has probably teased the wits out of the Champagne Charlies at the hunt balls. There, that will soon dry off. You'll feel rather sticky, but it's the best I can do, and I'm not going to waste any of our precious water.'

'Th—thanks.' Eve flushed hotly at the ease with which he had read her mind. Men believed that it excited a girl, the thought of being at the mercy of a tough and ruthless character, and she didn't dare to look at Wade in case she actually felt a stirring of curiosity about what it would feel like if he suddenly flung her down in the rampant ferns and took her with all the forceful assurance with which he tackled everything.

'What are you wating for?' There was an edge to his voice. 'To find out what it's like to tease a ruffian in jungle cloth?'

'I don't go in for that sort of behaviour,' she said indignantly.

'I bet you don't.' His eyes swept her up and down.

'What else is there for someone like you, whose virginity had to be preserved for the highest bidder? There's little honesty in it, but a whole lot of tantalisation, only don't try it on with me, lady, or I'll teach you that on the rough side of the tracks we don't cheat.'

'How dare you!' Eve itched to slap his hard, cynical face.

'I'd dare, lady.'

'I just bet you would,' she retorted. 'You wouldn't have come within ten miles of the ethics of a gentleman.'

'I thought you had a taste of gentlemanly behaviour a few hours ago, when not one of that sort would offer you his seat on that plane, which by now is safely landed while we're standing here steaming in this heat.'

Eve flushed again, and hated him for his knack of striking clean to the bone and exposing the painful truth. 'The impulse to survive does away with politeness, I suppose,' she said.

'Now you're learning, foxfire,' he mocked.

'Foxfire?' Her eyes ran enquiringly over his hard face.

'Didn't your elegant young man ever tell you that your hair matches the coat of the vixen as she streaks across the turf pursued by the hounds and the gallant huntsmen?'

James ... tell her that? Eve doubted if he'd ever noticed anything about her beyond that she dressed, spoke and behaved correctly, and would in due course inherit some sizeable stocks and shares.

'If your nerves have quite settled,' Wade drawled, 'we'll be falling in line again and might make another mile or so before you wilt and have to be fed.'

'I'm not an infant, Major O'Mara. I'll keep up with

you, don't worry about that. I'm just as eager as you are to reach civilisation.'

'Right. And next time a bird's egg falls on you, don't scream the forest down.'

'Did I upset your nerves?' she asked tartly.

'My nerves are iron, lady, but you could have been heard and the female scream can't be mistaken for anything but what it is, probably one of the most primitive sounds on earth.'

This time Eve thought it wise to let him have the final word, and taking hold of her bamboo stick and her bits and pieces wrapped in the plaid robe, she fell in behind him and they continued on their way ... into the very heart of the jungle, or so it seemed.

It was, Eve reflected, like being a pickle in a salad; the vegetation was all shades of green, except when a sudden bract of bougainvillea sprang vividly to life against the foliage, or a great stem of wild orchids burst forth from the trunk of a towering tree. The leaves of the plantain were enormous and could have served as umbrellas should it suddenly start to rain. Branches twisted together in the most erotic shapes, like dark limbs entwined in eternal passion, sometimes modestly veiled by drapes of lacy green fern.

Every now and again a bird would flutter down on large wings and startle Eve, or a parakeet would let out a raucous squawking sound, as if scolding the two human beings for being in a place meant for more primitive creatures.

The Major waded on through the moist, riotous, earthy-scented jungle with all the aplomb of a man taking a hike through Epping Forest with the prospect of a long cool beer awaiting him at the Rising Sun. Hack, hack, went his sharp-bladed *panga*, shearing through the thick stems and tangles of vine, lopping off the great leaves across their path, and tramping down with his boots the thorny growth that could have torn Eve's ankles.

Occasionally he shot a look at her, or flung a question over his khaki-clad shoulder. 'How're you coping, lady?'

'I'm having a picnic,' she rejoined. 'I'm wondering how anyone could join a jungle army to endure this ... whoever uses your services must pay well.'

'They pay sufficiently,' he said. 'Enough to put my kid through college.'

'Y-you have a family?' His casual reference to a child almost sent Eve sprawling into a patch of spiky bamboo, which she avoided just in time.

'A son.' He whacked away with his *panga* at a whip-like branch.

'Aren't you worried that you'll be killed?' she asked that broad back, with the dark patch of sweat between the shoulder-blades. 'That wouldn't do him much good, would it?'

'It's the worriers who get the bullet, so I steer clear of worrying.'

'What about your wife?' Eve swallowed drily. 'Surely she doesn't approve of the way you earn your living.'

'She was never the worrying sort,' he rejoined. 'Larry, the boy, is keen to be a doctor, and I intend to see to it that he gets what he wants.'

'How old is he?'

She heard Wade O'Mara emit a sardonic laugh. 'Nineteen, which makes him only a year younger than you, eh?'

'Yes,' she admitted, and her eyes swept the lean,

lithe, and forceful figure in front of her and she decided that Major O'Mara was in very good shape for a man with a grown-up son. How old had he been when the boy was born—about twenty? And was his wife attractive? Yes, Eve decided. This tough mercenary would like his woman to be feminine and rather helpless, with big blue eyes and fair hair in contrast to his darkness.

That was the image Eve built in her mind of the woman who waited for Wade O'Mara back in England, while he risked his neck in order to earn sufficient for his son's medical training. Eve thought of some of the men who were contemporaries of her guardian, and the kind of cash they played with on the investment market, able to pick up the phone and give instructions to a stockbroker involving thousands of pounds ... but the man who was dedicated to getting her safely to the Tanga coast had to kill in order to educate his son.

Eve felt rather shaken, as she had at the age of fifteen when a school friend had enlightened her about the production of babies ... as if she had learned a fact of life which was amazing and very intriguing. In the large house of her guardian she had been rather sheltered, and it had never been explained to her that men and women didn't only look and behave differently, but had a function in life that was also very dissimilar and accounted for the fact that men had aggressive ways to which women submitted either willingly or unwillingly.

Eve realised how aggressive was the jungle soldier whom she had to obey, on whose strength and ability she had to rely if she hoped to get to Tanga safe and well.

All around them seethed the forces of nature, and any one of the massive trees or tangled growths of vine could have been hiding the kind of menace he was trained to overcome. Without him she would be totally lost and at the mercy of all sorts of danger ... a cold shiver ran over Eve's moist skin, and never before had she felt so aware of being a woman as in this jungle with a tough mercenary who hunted rebels so that he could provide for his son.

What kind of a man did he become when he was back in England with the woman who was the mother of his son? Eve tried to resist the question, but it took a grip on her thoughts ... was he a very ardent lover, showing his hard white teeth in a possessive smile as he took into his hard brown arms the woman from whom he was parted for hazardous months on the other side of the world?

Was she aware that he sometimes had to rescue nuns from an endangered mission, and be responsible for escorting a lone girl through rebel-occupied country?

Or didn't he talk about the dangers of his job ... or the temptations involved?

Eve was shocked by her own thoughts, but they persisted in tormenting her as she tramped along in the wake of this man ... so mocking and sure of his masculinity ... and with a son named Larry. What could possibly be tempting in a man who antagonised her as much as this one did? A man who was married and the type she would have avoided in the normal course of events?

It was at that point in her feverish thoughts that Eve suddenly stumbled in her over-large sandals and gave a cry as her left foot turned over painfully. 'Damnation!' Wade O'Mara halted instantly and swung round, his black brows joined together above his blade of a nose. 'What have you done now?'

'N—nothing,' she said, but there were tears of pain dampening the edges of her eyes and she was obviously limping. He didn't move and when she drew level with him, he caught hold of her arm.

'I—I'm all right,' she insisted.

'Don't be a heroine until you have to be,' he growled. 'Let me have a look at the damage.'

'It's just a wrench——'

'Hoist the leg on this fallen log and let me look!'

It was a definite order and Eve reluctantly obeyed him. He removed her sandal and this added to her feeling of defencelessness, induced by the strength of his shoulders and the feel of his hand massaging her ankle.

He glanced at her and slitted his eyes against a ray of reddish sun coming down through an opening in the trees. 'You've done well for a slip of a girl, and this had better be rested for the night. I think we'll make camp, and then get an early start in the morning.'

Sympathy from the ruthless was bound to take a girl by surprise, and Eve stared down at her ankle clasped in his tough brown hand. She blinked in an effort to stop the tears from coming. 'Thanks,' she mumbled. 'That sun up there is going all to flame—I hadn't realised how the day was going.'

He glanced at the dark-strapped watch on his hairy wrist. 'The days start early in this part of the world and the nights come quickly. Yes, we'll now make camp, and I'm going to take a chance and light a small fire so we can have some tea. Fancy that?'

'Oh yes,' she said fervently.

A slight smile curled his lips, and for the briefest

moment his fingers seemed to move in a caress against the fine bones of her slim ankle. Then he put her sandal back on and latched it, and even as Eve was steadying herself with a hand on the hard bone and sinew of his shoulder, her heart was reacting in a most unsteady way.

CHAPTER THREE

By the time the Major had settled on their camp site, the sun had slid beyond the trees and dropped away into the gullies of shadow. Eve glanced around her and became aware of the primitive atmosphere of the jungle when the sun faded and the darkness fell like a cloak. The tall trees seemed to come closer and the sounds in the undergrowth grew menacing.

Though she had been at the mission just over two months, Eve had never spent a night in the actual jungle ... least of all with a man. She felt scared and strung-up, half fascinated by the experience, and yet wary of the man and the reason for the two of them being here, in the shadowy depths of this vast, unnerving and primeval place.

He had said he was going to light a fire, but Eve knew how risky that could be at night when the flickering flames might be seen, bringing upon them a sudden attack from out of the dark, sharp blades swinging in the firelight, doing to them what had been done to a Jesuit priest and several of his flock at a mission not far from the one where Eve had worked with Sister Mercy and the other nuns.

She waited in the deepening dusk, alone for the moment because Wade O'Mara had said he smelled creek water and had gone to investigate. Eve longed to sit down, but didn't dare risk it. Her ankle was aching, but it was the bodily weariness that was making her feel so nervous and wan. Oh, how lovely right now to have a bed to fall into, where she could snuggle under the duvet and sink her head into a soft pillow. Sheer luxury! And when she awoke a shower to stand under, lathering herself with a foamy soap, twisting about under the delicious cascade until her skin was glowing.

Eve came out of her reverie to find Wade O'Mara in the clearing. He was carrying some objects which made a thumping noise when he dropped them. 'Stones from the creekside,' he explained. 'I'll build the fire inside them and it won't be so visible.'

'Is it wise?' she asked. 'Perhaps we shouldn't risk it.'

'You need some hot sweet tea, my lady, and so do I as a matter of fact. I'll open a can of corned beef and we have some biscuits. We shan't do too badly, eh?'

'You're very casual about everything, aren't you?' Yet even as she spoke Eve couldn't help wondering what lay behind that imperturbable manner of his; was it military training which induced it, or was he concerned not to let her see just how grim their situation was; two people alone like this in alien country, his nerve and that Breda automatic shotgun all that stood between them and the bloodthirsty vengeance the rebels were wreaking upon anyone who stood in their path.

'What do you mean by casual?' Wade went down on his haunches and started to arrange the fire stones. He glanced up a moment and she caught the glimmer of his teeth and eyes ... alert as a leopard, she thought, with his vitality still at a high level of voltage despite the hard slogging pace he had set for both of them, all that day.

'Well, as if you did this kind of thing every night of your life.'

'I do it quite often, make camp in the jungle. The one definite difference is that I don't usually have the debutante of the season to share my bully beef and biscuits.'

'I wish you wouldn't keep bringing that up!' she exclaimed. 'I'm not a debutante any more—I didn't want to be one in the first place, but my guardian insisted.'

'Come now, I'm sure you enjoyed every moment of the admiration and the proposals.' His tone of voice was lazily sardonic. 'How many did you collect?'

Eve heard the branches of dry wood snapping in his hands as he laid the fire in the compact circle of stones, and she wished he wouldn't be so sarcastic when she was feeling too weary to enjoy answering him back.

'I forget,' she sighed. 'They were unimportant.'

'All but one of them, eh? You said you had a young man in England.'

'Did I?' Eve ran her fingers through her sweaty hair and pulled at the collar of her shirt. She wished she could have a wash, and wondered if the creek held sufficient water for a quick plunge.

'I feel so messy.' she said. 'I—I'm not asking for any of our drinking water, but would it be possible for me to bathe in the creek?'

'Utterly impossible.' he replied curtly. 'This is night-time, if you haven't noticed, and I don't know what's swimming about in there. You'll have to wait till the morning and I'll decide then if you can take a wash in it—it will be pretty muddy anyway.'

'Mud is good for the complexion,' she said flippantly. 'What could be in it beside mud?'

'Things with teeth that snap at pink toes and milky-white bottoms,' he rejoined. 'I know you aren't feeling your usual bandbox self, but it's better to be safe than nipped, wouldn't you say?'

'I suppose so.' But she said it regretfully and watched as a match flared and was applied quickly to the kindling he had laid. The acrid tang of woodsmoke filled the night air and small flames fluttered upwards, then gradually sank to feed on the dry branches. Wade unbuckled the straps of his knapsack and took out a couple of cans, something tightly rolled, and finally a kettle that would hold about two cups of water. Eve listened as the water gurgled from the leather bottle into the small kettle, and she reflected again how unruffled this man seemed to be. She was glad he was so tough and self-reliant, but at the same time he was so disturbing and awoke in her a feeling of being a helpless and vulnerable female. She should be the one making the tea, yet it was he who placed the kettle on the improvised stove and put chunks of sugar in a large enamel mug.

'We'll have to share this,' he said, and the firelight showed her the deep groove in his hard, unshaven cheek. 'Like a loving cup in those romantic stories you probably read in bed.'

'I'm not a romantic fool,' she snapped. 'You enjoy getting at me, don't you, just for the fun of it because I'm keeping you from what you really enjoy!'

'And what might that be?' he drawled, busily at work with a can opener, also found in the cavernous depths of his knapsack. 'From what I know of men—and at my age, with my experience, I presume to know a little more than you, my lady—this situation has elements to it that most men would enjoy. I'm not so very different from all those guys, but this isn't a regular sort of picnic, honey, and while you and I strike tinder and make sparks, you don't let your thoughts wander where they shouldn't.'

'And where's that, may I ask?' Eve couldn't control a rush of colour to her cheeks, for he seemed to be implying that she was getting romantic ideas about him.

'All around us, in the jungle,' he said explicitly. 'We both know what could come out of there if our fire is spotted, and it's best not to think of what I'd have to do rather than see you fall into their hands—presuming it's true what you hinted, that I enjoy the business of killing.'

Eve stared at him, a hand clenching her side as the kettle boiled and he dropped into it a handful of tea from a tin.

'Sorry we haven't any milk,' he said drily, 'but the tea will be hot and sweet and invigorating.'

'Do you mean'—she could feel her heart thumping, 'you'd kill me?'

'Sure, rather than see happen to you what I've seen elsewhere. My dear deb. I'm not in this man's army for kicks, or completely for the cash. People are being butchered out here, good people on the whole, if a little misguided about how other folks' countries should be run. I've seen nasty things in the last couple of years, and as I said once before, you should have stayed at home and married that smooth young man of yours, then you wouldn't be stuck with me in the middle of a jungle—a guy who may have to blow your pretty head off rather than see it chopped off.'

'Ugh!' Eve shuddered all the way to the bottom of her spine. 'You don't spare the rod, do you?'

'It had to be said, and now stop thinking about it.' He untied the bundle he had taken from his knapsack and it sprang free of its tapes, an army blanket that was waterproofed on one side, which he laid on the ground he had firmly trampled down with his boots. 'Come on, sit down and try and relax. Do you like corned beef?'

She nodded, and despite his horrific words she wasn't turned off the food, which he handed to her on a chipped enamel plate, with a few digestive biscuits on the side. 'Thank you.' She glanced up at him, standing very tall in the firelight. 'And don't hesitate to do it, if you have to!'

'A proficient soldier never hesitates, and I'm very proficient when I have to be. Also a good shot, if that will set your mind at rest?'

'My mind's at rest.' In the shifting glow of the fire, as he poured the tea, his features were distinctly ruthless and above them he had the tousled dark hair of a freebooter. Eve was in no doubt that she could be sure of swift annihilation should the rebels attack them, and even as she felt a sense of relief about it, she still felt that deep-down sense of disturbance at being so alone with Wade O'Mara. She had never met anyone of his type before. Had he always been a soldier, wandering from war to war, and never at home long enough to become tamed and ordinary like so many other husbands? Was his wife so undemanding that she didn't mind being without this tough, resourceful man for months on end?

'Thank you, Major.' Eve accepted the big tea mug and set her lips to the brim. The tea was strong, but she was far too thirsty to mind, and she gulped her half of the brew while he sprawled on the blanket and crunched a biscuit while he watched her.

'One thing I'll say for you, young deb, you don't make a fuss about eating and drinking like a soldier. Thanks.' He accepted the mug and tipped it to his own

40

mouth, and Eve could have sworn that he set his lips exactly where hers had been. Oh heavens, she thought, and came to the realisation that there was an insidious, very masculine charm under the veneer of hardness that this mercenary Major presented to the world in general. She recalled his firmness in getting the nuns aboard the last plane to Tanga, and the way he had briefly smiled at Sister Mercy.

'Are you a Catholic?' she asked him abruptly.

'I was born into the faith,' he replied, tossing corned beef into his mouth and munching with appetite. 'It isn't often that I get to practise its tenets, as you can see from the uniform I wear. Why do you ask?'

'You were very kind to Sister Mercy and the other nuns, and I noticed that once or twice you used Latin terms that she understood.'

'And I don't strike you as being normally kind, eh?'

'I—I wouldn't say that.' Eve glanced at the fire and chewed her own supper. 'I'm glad we have a fire, but it still scares me in case it gives us away.'

'You don't have to be scared,' he drawled. 'You won't know what's hit you.'

'All the same—well, we've both got a lot to live for, haven't we? You have your son, and I—I have my life back in England.'

'With the honourable young man who allowed you to come out here to scrub floors and risk your neck?' A black eyebrow arched above cynical grey eyes, which dwelt on the fine gold chain and golden good-luck coin which she wore, glinting in the firelight against the smooth skin of her throat. 'Were you testing him, honey? Hoping he'd dash after you and grab you off the airfield before you boarded the plane?'

Eve thought bitterly of James the last time she had dined with him, eating expensively at the Charisse before they went on to the theatre ... she had told him she was thinking of coming here, but he had laughed away the idea. 'Don't be a silly girl,' he had said, patting her hand as if she were an infant or his doddering aunt, but never a girl he hoped to sweep off her feet with his love-making. 'Whatever would you find to do out in the bush? A little orchid-picking, my sweet?'

She could have told Wade O'Mara that she despised James and thought him a useless stick, but wisdom prevailed and she smiled what she hoped was a yearning, romantic smile.

'I wanted to prove that I could be of use, and I have proved it.' she replied.

'You've proved to the hilt that you were running away from that exciting life of yours back in England. Of course you were, so don't deny it. If you were so keen to be of use to the community you could have applied for proper training at a hospital or taken a Cordon Bleu course in cooking and opened your own bistro ... both would have offered you the chance to scrub floors and peel potatoes.'

'You're a sarcastic devil!' Eve exclaimed. 'The cynicism is layers thick on your hide!'

'It probably is,' he agreed. 'But at least I'm honest about what drives me to do certain things. I don't wrap my motives in a self-deluding veil of sacrifice and service. You were bored to the hilt with being a social butterfly, so you decided to create a flutter by scorching your wings on the edge of a political flare-up. Only it turned out to be more like a forest fire and you didn't bargain for being caught in it with a stinging brute like me, did you?' The look he gave her was derisive and knowing. 'Hand me your plate, Eve. You've earned a sweet even if it's too late for a spanking.'

'No doubt that's how you've dealt with your son,' she said, 'when you've been at home to deal with his training.'

'No doubt,' he drawled. 'Come on, I've opened a can of pineapple chunks and I'm fairly sure you have a sweet tooth, not having arrived at the stage when you need to trim any surplus fat from that sylph-like figure; and believe me, by the time I've dragged you through the jungle, like Tarzan and Jane, you'll be trim enough to be a model.'

Setting her lips and refusing to be humoured, Eve handed him her plate, for the truth was she was still quite hungry but she knew he had to preserve as much of their solid food as he could. She certainly wasn't averse to sharing the pineapple chunks, but his caustic remarks took some swallowing ... maybe because he struck too close to the truth for comfort. It wasn't until she had arrived at the mission and found there was real need for her services that she had faced the truth of why she had come. It had been her act of rebellion against a cushioned yet controlled life, and she had needed to get far away from England in order to feel free of her guardian's iron hand in the velvet glove. She was fond of him, and grateful to him for the way he had cared for her, but he expected to rule her life and plan her future, and Eve had fled in a sort of revolt a man like Wade O'Mara could never be expected to understand.

She doubted if Major O'Mara, sprawling there in his mercenary khaki, had ever felt a stab of fear in his entire life. No one had a lead on him, not even his wife. But Eve felt beholden to her guardian, though not yet was she going to be forced into marriage that would suit him far more than it would suit her. She had wanted to test her wings, but she wasn't complaining about the scorch marks, and with a tilt to her chin she accepted her plate of fruit chunks with a stiff murmur of thanks.

'Sorry there's no ice-cream to go with them,' he drawled, 'but I guess you can whip up enough ice for the two of us when you put on that frosty look.'

'Funny, aren't you?' Eve ate her pineapple from her fingers and thoroughly enjoyed doing so ... maybe in her secret heart she had longed to be a hoyden for a while, her feelings roughed up by a man who would never have been smooth with women. She could just imagine what she looked like with tangled hair, wearing slacks that flapped around her ankles and a shirt that was oily from insect repellent. Her guardian would have a fit, and James would probably swoon.

'That's it, smile.' The voice was as rough and purring as if it came from a leopard's throat. 'I won't ask you to share the joke, for I'm well aware that naughty thoughts can lurk behind a demure face.'

'I expect you presume to know all there is to know about women,' she rejoined, licking juice from her fingers. 'I don't doubt that in your travels as a warrior you've met every colour and every creed. Your wife must have a mind as broad as Loch Ness.'

'Broader,' he agreed, and the smile on his firelit face was an inscrutable one, making Eve wonder just how much his marriage meant to him. Like all the other thoughts he aroused it was a disturbing one ... she didn't want to delve into his private life, but they were

44

a man and woman alone in the primeval jungle and it would have been unnatural had she not been curious about him ... as he was probably curious about her.

Suddenly an ominous snarl came from the depths of the trees and Eve turned her head towards the sound and felt her heart give a leap. 'What's that?'

'Probably a leopard on the hunt for its supper,' he said casually.

'So long as it doesn't start fancying us,' she gasped.

'Let's hope it will soon find its kill. I don't want to use the rifle if I can avoid it, for a gunshot in the dark can carry for miles.'

Eve shivered, and realised anew how perilous their situation was. The fire had to be kept low in case the flames were seen and this increased the chance of some dangerous animal leaping upon them.

'Don't start getting jittery,' he said. 'Leopards are the least of our worries. Have you ever seen one?'

'One or two used to roam about in the vicinity of the mission, but there was a fence of pointed stakes around the compound.'

'Lovely creatures,' he murmured, 'with a spring to them like oiled silk. Too bad they're hunted for their skins.'

'I hate real fur coats,' she said, recalling with a flash to her eyes a quarrel she had once had with her guardian when he had tried to make her wear a sealskin jacket he had bought for her birthday. 'I can't bear the thought of animals being slaughtered just to satisfy the vanity of women and the ego of the men who buy furs for them.'

'Do you know how they kill the leopards so the lovely supple skins won't be marked?' Wade was rolling himself a cigarette from his pouch of tobacco, and he shot her a look across the guarded flames of their fire, his brows a single dark slash above his eyes.

'In some beastly cruel way. I expect.' Eve met his eyes. 'Have you ever hunted them?'

He shook his head. 'Would you care for a cigarette?' he asked. 'Hand-rolled, but they serve.'

'I don't smoke, thank you.' She watched as he took a glowing stick from the fire and lit the cigarette between his lips; the flame played a moment over his features and she thought again how ruthless he looked and yet there was a side to him that was far more subtle and complex, as if cruelty migh repe' him. 'Major, did you fight in Biafra?' she aske d or impulse.

'Yes.' He slung the stick on to the fire and leaned back on the blanket his eyes narrowed against the smoke of the cigarett ir the corner of his mouth.

'It must have been horrible.'

'It was.'

'Those fearful massacres! We read about them in the newspapers.'

'They weren't a pretty sight,' he agreed. 'But you don't want nightmares and in a while we're going to settle down for the night.'

Eve glanced around her at the density of the jungle trees, at what might be lying in wait to pounce upon them while they slept.

'I sleep like a cat,' he drawled, 'with one eye open. You'll be safe enough with me.'

'Will I?' The words sprang of themselves to her lips, and for some reason they sounded—provocative, so that instantly Eve could have bitten her tongue.

'The fact that you're an attractive wench cuts little

46

ice with me,' he said, a trifle cuttingly. 'Apart from the fact that you were with those nuns, I don't happen to seduce girls young enough to be my. daughter. Does that relieve your girlish apprehensions?'

Eve was grateful for the darkness which concealed the colour that rushed into her cheeks. 'I didn't mean——'

'Didn't you?' Smoke curled about his dark head. 'I'm a soldier and I fight wars, and when the opportunity offers I relax—with a woman. I don't happen to regard this situation as a very relaxing one, and when we do kip down for the night I'm going to give you a tablet that will relieve any aches and sprains and make you sleep easy, so you'll dream for a few hours that you're back in your cosy canopied bed at the family mansion, which I daresay stands in its own acres, with enough land a man might farm without breaking his back.'

'You sound as if you might be a frustrated farmer,' she murmured. 'Is that your ambition, if you don't get a bullet in your back?'

'Who taught you perception?' he queried, squinting across the fire through his pungent cigarette smoke.

'Maybe I was born with it,' she said. 'Even debutantes aren't necessarily feather-brained.'

'No, the only thing that's feathery about you, lady, is that you're such a fledgling in a hard cruel world. You'll grow up, more's the pity.'

'Why is it a pity, Major?'

'Kids I find amusing, even those with plenty of backchat, but women have only one function as far as I'm concerned.'

'What ghastly cynicism!' she exclaimed. 'How did

you ever come to get married with your outlook on—love?'

'There are a couple of specific reasons why a man puts his head into that particular noose, so can't you guess? I was doing my National Service and I met this fetching little waitress in the canteen. As I don't happen to believe in abortion I became a husband at the age of nineteen, and a proud father at twenty. Let me add that I've no regrets on that score, and now are you satisfied that you've winkled my secret out of me?'

'I—I wasn't being inquisitive,' she denied, and it was curious how unshocked she was by his revelation. Somehow she had guessed that this tough, resilient character had never been romantically in love ... it was there in his face, in his eyes that he placed women in two categories, those to be revered like Sister Mercy, and those to be desired like the girl he had got into trouble during his very first year as a soldier. It touched Eve that he had done the honourable thing and was so obviously proud of the son from his enforced marriage. Her fingers clenched in the blanket on which she sat, almost as if she were controlling an impulse to reach out and run her fingers down his lean life-clawed face. Heaven help her, it wouldn't be wise to touch him ... as that other Eve had touched Adam when the serpent whispered.

'You shivered just then,' he said. 'Beginning to feel cold? That does happen in the jungle at night.'

'I—I guess I'm tired,' she gave a little yawn. 'It's been a long and very unusual day.'

'It has, at that.' He leapt with agility to his feet and tossed his cigarette butt into the fire. 'You'll want to go into the bush to spend a penny, so you'd better take my torch. Keep the light trained downwards, won't you?'

'Of course.' Romantic he wasn't, but he was certainly to be trusted not to take a girl for a plastic doll without natural functions which needed to be relieved. She accepted the torch with a murmur of thanks, and was so terribly glad he wasn't like James, who went turkey-red when a girl excused herself to go to the powder-room. There in the jungle bush she tried not to think about snakes and knobbly black spiders and concentrated on how James would react if he could see her right now. When she returned to the fireside she was smiling to herself.

'Something tickle your fancy?' Wade enquired drily.

'Oh, I was just wondering how they'd react back home if they could see me now.'

'So it amuses you that the guardian and the boyfriend would probably be shocked?' As he spoke he was delving into his knapsack and Eve saw the glimmer of something white in his hands. 'The boy-friend might have grounds for breaking off the engagement if he knew you were alone in the primitive jungle with a mercenary, eh?'

'We aren't yet officially engaged,' she said, and watched as strong, deft hands unfurled a length of filmy mosquito netting.

'But it's on the cards, eh? The desirable union of the season's deb with a young man capable of handling your inheritance if not your imagination.'

'My imagination, Major O'Mara, is no more vivid than anyone else's.'

'I beg to differ. You're standing there right now and

having mental images of sharing this blanket and net with me. Dare you deny it?'

'I—I had come to that conclusion,' she admitted, feeling the warmth come into her cheeks as she envisioned herself tucked in close to that lean and ruthless body ... she had never been that close to a friend, let alone a stranger.

'And as your imagination is female, Eve, you've gone a step further and petrified yourself with the belief that a rough soldier is going berserk the moment he comes in contact with your nubile young body. It could happen, along with a lot of other things that might happen before I get you to Tanga in one piece, but you're going to have to take a chance, like the one you took when you told that pilot you could trek it with me. You knew when you spoke up that I wasn't a weed among the coronets.'

'I was aware of the risks I was running,' she said, a trifle breathlessly. 'It was more important to me that Sister Mercy and her nuns be flown to safety—I happen to mean that! I might be a bit spoiled, but I'm not selfish!'

'There's no need to be on the defensive with me,' he drawled. 'I know a lot more about women than you'll ever know about men, so let's get something straight. When a man makes love, just about everything else goes out of his head and he becomes almighty vulnerable. I can't afford that happy state of being right now, with leopards and rebels on the prowl. Do I make myself clear?'

'As glass,' she said, and could feel her cheeks burning.

'Right.' He held out his hand and there on the palm

of it was a small round object. 'Swallow this and you'll sleep through without being worried about me or anything else. Go on, take it.'

Eve accepted the tablet and put it against the edge of her tongue. 'I—I think I might sleep without it,' she said nervously.

'You'll take it,' he rejoined. 'I want you fighting fit in the morning, with no residue of pain from that ankle you turned over. The tablet has something in it to relax your nerves and ease your aches, and I'd take one myself except that I've got to keep alert and not fall into a deep sleep. D'you want a sip of water to help it go down?'

'Please.'

He poured a little of their water into the mug and handed it to her. Eve made no further protest and swallowed the tablet. She had to trust him ... there was no one else around to see after her, and even to look into the density of the jungle was to feel the nerves crawling in her stomach. The trees were black creaking shapes in the darkness and there were stealthy sounds that made her skin creep.

Wade handed her the netting and told her she was to swathe herself in it. 'Like an oriental bride,' he drawled wickedly, 'right over your head and face. Go on. You won't suffocate, but it will keep out anything that might crawl on you in the night.'

'Oh, do you have to be so explicit?' she appealed. 'What are you going to use to cover yourself, or don't you care about the crawlies?'

'I can wrap this around my head like granddad's nightcap.' He showed her the white silk scarf which he had confiscated at the airfield bungalow.

'So that's why you wanted it!'

'Sure. Did you imagine I was saving it for a night out at the country club?'

Eve grinned as she began to twirl the netting about herself. 'I can't imagine you at the country club drinking gin slings and talking about the latest polo match. I think that would bore you to distraction.'

'And what can you imagine me doing in my spare time?' he asked, and he was down on his haunches banking the fire with half-dried mosses and leaves which he had gathered from the edge of the clearing.

'Riding,' she said instantly, 'but not in any kind of local pack. And you probably play a lot of squash.'

'How come you say that?'

'You haven't a pot, have you?'

He stood up, tall and hard from his chin to his heels. 'I'm not quite in my dotage, kitten, but I guess thirty-nine must seem pretty ancient to you.'

'No——'

'Come off it,' he said derisively. 'I have a son not much younger than you, and if I haven't a stomach that's gone to pot, then you can put it down to the hard graft of being a soldier. Oh, sure, I'm called a mercenary, but most of us are hard-bitten characters from the regular army who, for some reason or other, find ourselves fighting in the jungle or the desert. It isn't just the cash, but when you've been a soldier for most of your life, it comes easier to answer a call to action than to sign on at the foundry or the factory. Three years ago I was in Belfast, in charge of a bomb disposal squad. Four of us got blown about one night, and when I came out of hospital they discharged me from the army. I tried to settle down to civvies, but it didn't work. And now I'm here in the jungle with you, lady. Funny old life, isn't it?'

She nodded, and wondered how his wife had taken it when he had put away his civvy suit and put on a uniform once again. She supposed it was like a drug, the danger he had lived with all these years. Even the domestic comforts had not been strong enough to hold him.

'You actually enjoy all this, don't you?' she said.

Wade shrugged his shoulders and came over to inspect how efficiently Eve had swathed herself in the netting. He shook his head at her. 'You look like a kid dressed up in mother's net curtains,' he said. 'Come here, I want this stuff over your hair, neck, face and arms, otherwise you'll wake up in the morning with bites and welts all over you, not to mention a dose of incipient malaria.'

Eve stood there and allowed herself to be covered up until she did indeed resemble a Persian bride. She gave a throaty little laugh, and tried to ignore his hand as it smoothed the netting down over her body.

'What's so funny?' he asked. 'Or are you naturally ticklish?'

'I feel like a novice about to take vows,' she said, for it seemed wiser not to refer to a bridal image.

'Vows of chastity?' he drawled. 'You're not the type.'

'Oh, how come you're so sure?' she asked. 'You've only known me a day, yet you presume to judge my character as if we're old—friends.'

'It is a safer word, isn't it?' he jeered, adjusting the netting so that her neck was well covered. 'Any

53

guy who called himself your friend would be a poor stick.'

'Thanks!'

'I'm paying you a compliment, you half-child.' He gazed down at her, making her aware of his lean height and the total self-assurance of a man who had been to dangerous places and faced all kinds of hazards. 'I have reverence for nuns and I admire their courage and dedication, but be thankful you aren't driven by their needs. Your sort will be far more—enjoyable.'

With James? The unwelcome thought flashed through her mind even as her eyes measured this man's shoulders and her skin tingled from his touch.

'There, I think you're sufficiently mummified for the night. I haven't wrapped the netting too tightly about your neck, have I? The neck is a particularly vulnerable and tasty part of the anatomy so far as gnats and s'quitoes are concerned.' He let go of her and started to search his pockets for something. He brought out a length of string and proceeded to cut it in two with his knife. 'Now we'll tie up the cuffs of your trousers in case a snake decides to warm himself inside them.'

'Do you have to be so—so precise?' she begged.

'Snakes aren't stupid, you know. They like to warm themselves against soft young skin, so if you feel something snuggling up to you——'

'I'm to presume it's a snake?'

'What else would it be?' Eve knew as he haunched down and tied the flapping cuffs of her pants that his mouth was quirked at one side in a wicked little smile. Oh, he'd look after her to the very best of his ability, and he'd get her to Tanga if he could, but he wasn't going to deny himself the pleasure of teasing and tantalising her. She was a new sort of experience for him, and she didn't believe for one moment that he regarded her from a paternal angle. His remarks were a little too risqué for that, and somehow he didn't strike her as the type of man to be all that fatherly, even with his own son.

'There, that should keep you fairly secure from the snakes and other pests,' he said.

'Do you include yourself in that list?' she asked.

'Almighty curious about my amorous inclinations, aren't you, lady?' He lifted an eyebrow and gave her a look that was just on the edge of being derisive. 'It's partly your age, and partly the situation that we're in, so you thank your stars I realise it and don't take your pert remarks for a come-on.'

Eve bit her lip and wondered if there was something about this tough mercenary that appealed to instincts deep within her, stirred into life by the dense tropical night and the untamed forces of the jungle. He was so much a part of those forces, with a danger to him that was intensified by their primitive surroundings.

The uniform he wore, and the alert discipline of his mind and body, were indicative of what he was trained to do ... to overcome a silent enemy and kill in several savage ways if he had to. It was awful for Eve to contemplate, but at the same time it was exciting.

And because of that sense of excitement she was suddenly very wary of him ... and of herself.

'Ready for bed?' he asked. 'I want to make an early start and try to get to Tanga some time tomorrow.'

She nodded and tried not to notice that her feelings

55

went a little bleak ... at Tanga they would part and go their separate ways. She to board a plane for England, while he would rejoin his unit in some other part of this rebel-torn country. And back in England her guardian would reinforce his argument that she marry James and settle down to a cosy, unexciting and predictable life. It wouldn't matter to anyone that she didn't love James. He was from a good family and he was a kind, undemanding young man. As her guardian had said, she ought to regard herself as a very lucky young woman.

Lucky? Eve shut her mind to all that, and glanced down at the army blanket which her present guardian was smoothing out beside the low-burning fire in its nest of stones, wafting into the air the acrid tang of woodsmoke.

Ever afterwards when she smelled leaves burning in a wood somewhere, she would think of her flight through the jungle with a mercenary Major, who placed his knapsack for a pillow and indicated that she settle down for the night.

'Near the fire,' he said, 'so you'll keep warm.'

When she hesitated, he raised an eyebrow and silently watched her until she took the place he indicated. He settled the netting around her and wrapped her lower body in the plaid robe. 'Comfortable?' he asked.

'Yes—thank you.'

'Right.' He stood a long moment looking about him, tensed in every nerve for any sound that might not be made by a natural denizen of the jungle. She heard a sliding movement and saw something steely glint in the firelight ... it was the broad lethal blade of the *panga* which he drew from its leather sheath and placed at his side when he settled down at her side. His shotgun was actually on the blanket between them ... like the ancient sword of knightly honour, she thought drowsily, there to defend her as if she were his lady fair.

She felt him stretch out and rest his head on the knapsack beside her own head. The white scarf he had twisted loosely about his neck and face and Eve had to bite on her knuckles to suppress a sudden nervous giggle.

'Go to sleep,' he ordered, 'and give that vivid imagination of yours a rest for the night.'

'I—I was just thinking how odd we must look, Major.'

'There's no one to see us except the monkeys,' he rejoined, 'and they won't tell on us. I hope that young man of yours won't think the worse of you for having to bed down for the night with a rough and ready soldier. Is he the tolerant type?'

Eve suspected that James would be shocked to his marrow to learn of her night in the jungle with a tough mercenary, some of whom had the reputation of being less than honourable when it came to women. He would be bound to suspect the worst, but she didn't mind. She had never wanted to marry him ... now she could feel herself actively recoiling from the idea of belonging to him. He'd probably find it difficult coping with being lost on Hampstead Heath.

'Well, don't worry.' This time the Major had not been able to read her thoughts, maybe because he was lying on his back instead of looking into her eyes. 'By the time you get back to good old Blighty, this will seem like a dream you had and you can invent a story he'll swallow without being awkward. Goodnight, *ndito*.'

'Goodnight, *bwana*.'

Eve heard him laugh softly to himself, for in the Masai language he had called her his girl, and she had called him her boss.

CHAPTER FOUR

Eve woke suddenly and lay absorbing the strangeness of it all. The fire had died, for no longer did those tendrils of acrid smoke drift upwards. She turned her head very carefully and dragged the mosquito netting away from her face ... the Major lay deeply asleep, his black hair tousled, his chin and jaws dark with his beard. Eve had a feeling he had kept awake most of the night, but now as dawn crept into the sky he allowed himself the luxury of an hour's sleep.

She didn't intend to wake him, and with extreme care she rose to her feet and disentangled herself from the rest of the net, bundling it and setting it to one side. Then she turned to the small pile of articles she had confiscated from that circular suitcase which the pilot had obligingly left behind. A bar of soap, a sponge and a towel were gathered up, and with a final glance at that sleeping figure to make sure he wasn't foxing her, Eve made for the tree-shadowed path that led in the direction of the creek.

If there was one thing she just had to have it was a plunge into water and a good lathering of soap to help make her feel fresh and human again.

This was like playing truant, as if she were a schoolgirl again, and Eve smiled to herself and reckoned that if she were quick she could be bathed and dressed and back at their camp site before the Major awoke and could alarm her with reasons why she shouldn't bathe in the creek.

She breathed the cool morning air and felt the spell of a slumbrous quiet that would last until the sun began to spread its flame across the treetops. She heard rustlings and the occasional bird call, and gazed in wonder at the yards of moss hanging down from the forks of trees, along with ribbons of fern. Several enormous webs glinted with the thick dew that had made their recent occupants retreat into the underbrush. Eve firmly closed her mind to anything unpleasant, and a few minutes later had emerged on to the banks of the creek. A mist lay over the peat-coloured water, and there was a cluster of blue lotus at the edge where she stood, their petals closed into a big bud, waiting for the sun to open them on the big green leaves.

Eve hung her towel on a lower branch of a massive, mottled tree whose roots stretched out into the water, swiftly removed her clothes and hung them with equal care on another of the branches. Then, nude as Phryne, with soap and sponge clutched in her hands, she ran out gleefully into the water and gave herself up to the bliss of bathing and splashing about, lost to everything but the need to feel clean and fresh.

Above the treetops the rising sun had become a ball of flame, and a flock of green birds rose in unison against the red-gold sky. The mud banks, however, had begun to give off a rank smell which Eve ignored, and from the jungle came the chattering and scolding of monkeys in the high crowns of the trees as they swung back and forth on the long chains of creepers thick as an arm.

She'd enjoy a few more minutes in the water, which

despite its leaf-dyed colour had made her feel tingling clean, then she would have to dress and return to the camp site. Suddenly she felt the nerves knot in her stomach as she spotted a movement beyond the bank where she had left her clothes ... a figure swung out from among the trees and with long hairy arms grabbed at her belongings and carried them off.

Clad only in the wet sheen of her white skin and auburn hair, Eve realised with dismay that one of the more daring monkeys had decided to find out if her garments were edible ... oh lord, now she was in a naked predicament, with only a bar of soap and a sponge to keep her covered ... unless like that other Eve she got hold of a large leaf to cover herself!

With every passing second the jungle was coming noisily awake, and Eve realised that Wade O'Mara would be waking up as well, and he'd be furious when he found she had slipped away from his side to come and enjoy a forbidden bathe in the creek.

Furious he was ... she could see that the instant he strode from among the trees on to the mud bank. 'You damn little idiot,' he yelled across the water. 'You'll come out of there without delay, or I'll come in and drag you out!'

When she didn't move, his voice cracked like a whip. 'You crazy little fool, Eve! Can't you see this creek mud is crawling with crabs now that the sun is up?'

It was ... the rotted vegetation was moving and shifting as if alive and Eve felt her stomach turn over.

'I—I can't come out,' she half-choked. 'I have nothing on!'

'For heaven's sake! I've seen unclad females before

today, and I'm old enough to be your father! Come on out before the mud crabs make a meal of you!'

'M—my clothes,' she whimpered. 'A monkey took them——'

'That figures,' he said grimly, and as she watched he unbuttoned his khaki shirt and removed it, revealing a torso the colour of copper. He waded out into the water, holding open the shirt so she could dive into it.

'Come on, you little jackass!' he ordered.

Eve had no option but to obey him, and with her skin aflame with mortification she dashed towards him, flinging up water as he gathered her into the shirt and swung her up into his arms, so her bare white legs were out of reach of that mass of scurrying black crabs, clicking and snapping round his booted feet. He strode back with her to their camp site, along the pathway droning with flies. Eve's fingers clenched a warm coppery shoulder and never had she felt so helpless and vulnerable, all but bare in the steely arms of this angry man.

'You damn little jackass!' he said again.

'You're always so complimentary,' she mumbled.

'You deserve a good hiding where it would sting ... so you were going to emerge from the creek like Aphrodite of the foam, eh, glowingly clean and a real sweet meal for the crabs and the gnats?'

'I—I didn't expect a darned monkey to run off with my things,' she said. 'Whatever will I do?'

'You'll trek through the jungle wrapped in a blanket,' he replied, 'if I fail to find your shirt and trousers. Hasty little female, aren't you? I told you last night to stay away from the creek, but you had to wash yourself and smell like a lily. As if I care!'

'Well, I care,' she rejoined. 'I'm not one of your soldiers.'

'No,' he drawled, and she could feel him looking down at her, and again she felt an acute helplessness in his arms, with the dark hair curling down to his wrists, embedding the thick leather strap of his watch. There was such assurance to his strength, a careless male power, a saddle-tanning to his skin that seemed to make him impervious to what would bite her.

'We're quite the knight and the rescued maiden, aren't we?' he jeered. 'Lady, you just don't go bathing in a jungle creek as if you were taking a dip in the family pool, and from now on you'll do nothing except on my say-so. Do you hear me?'

'Your voice would carry across a parade ground,' she retorted. 'I bet the men under your command just love you!'

'Love?' He gave an abrupt laugh that startled a pair of sunbirds from their path. 'In this inhuman race to survive, honey, that commodity is now in very short supply. Human beings have become like the bird-eating spiders in this jungle.'

'Ugh!' Eve shuddered in his whipcord arms, lashed around her as he ducked beneath a curtain of ragged mosses and they entered the clearing where they had spent the night. 'Of course, one occasionally sees a white canary flying in the face of danger.'

'The Beauty and the Beast syndrome,' she murmured.

'Exactly.' He set her down on the khaki blanket. 'It's a fact of life.'

Eve pushed a damp strand of hair from her forehead and allowed herself a brief look at him. Did he understand that in her hunger to be clean the creek had taken on the look of a laguna in the dawn mist, hiding the things that slept in the mud? His eyes flicked the auburn dampness of her hair and fell to the tremulous redness of her mouth.

'I know darn well I can't treat you like a raw recruit,' he said, 'but I'm afraid you're going to have to smarm yourself in gnat repellent from your ears to your heels, so you'd better start now while I make a fire and cook us up some coffee and sausages.'

'Sausages?' she exclaimed, and became aware of another sort of hunger.

'I found a tin of them at the airfield bungalow, so we'll eat a good breakfast before setting off for Tanga.'

'What about my clothes, Major?' Eve bit her lip as the grey eyes scanned her slim figure in the khaki shirt that came to her thighs. His mouth quirked into that one-sided smile. 'At the moment you look cute in my shirt, lady, but I'd dread to imagine what you'd look like after several hours of slogging through jungle bamboo and flying *bitchos*. We'll have our breakfast, then I'll make a search for your things—dammit, Eve, we'll lose about an hour of our trek because of your female irresponsibility!'

'I—I'm sorry, Major.'

'That's all very well. You women hasten in where angels fear to fly, and then get all dewy-eyed with regret. You do realise that we're on the run from a pack of two-legged animals who would have a glorious time passing you around like candy?'

'You said—you promised——' She glanced significantly at his gun.

'Sure, but you'll recall, you little jackass, that I was taking a snooze when you sneaked off and took a bath in the creek. What would you have done had it not been a monkey who grabbed your clothes?'

'Screamed,' she said, with a shudder.

'Hoping I'd hear you, no doubt, with a jungle full of animals waking up for their breakfast. Well, come on, get yourself well anointed with insect repellent—and do put on that robe before I start getting ideas!'

'At this time of the morning, Major?' But she turned away instantly in search of the plaid robe, feeling the heat come into her skin. As she grabbed the robe and put it on she heard that short growl of a laugh issue from Wade O'Mara's throat.

'What's the time of day got to do with it?' he asked, as he went in search of wood that when stripped of its bark would be dry enough underneath to ignite without too much trouble.

After he had got the fire going and placed his smoke-blackened kettle on the stones, he opened the can of sausages, which to the delight of both of them were bedded in baked beans in a thick sauce. 'Manna from heaven,' he growled, and handing Eve a plate he prepared to tip half the contents of the can on to it.

'Cold?' she exclaimed.

'Can't be helped,' he said. 'I haven't a pan to heat them.'

'Can't you stand the can in the fire?' she asked. 'It would be nice to have a warm breakfast.'

'No doubt, if you don't mind it smoky?'

'A little smoke won't hurt me.'

'Not quite the hothouse orchid I took you for, eh?' He replaced the lid of the sausage can, dug a couple of holes in it with his opener and carefully settled it in the fire. He flicked a look over her and she tilted her chin, standing there in a man's robe trailing round her feet, her hair combed back damply from her temples.

'You look little more than a kid at the moment.'

'I expect I do,' she said, but inwardly she didn't feel like one. She was still wearing his shirt under the robe, and he was standing there palming coffee into the kettle, his torso tanned to the toughness of saddle leather, except for a puckered scar about six inches long in the region of his heart. She wanted to ask about it and decided that it had something to do with why he had been discharged from the regular army.

He saw her eyes upon his chest and his mouth gave a sardonic twist. 'A bit of metal from a bomb,' he informed her. 'It got bedded in me and spoiled my beauty. You're flinching, Eve, so it's just as well you can't see the one on the back of my left thigh.'

'And yet you enjoy being a soldier and can't stay away from a fight,' she said, and she was flinching at the thought of the white-hot metal ploughing its way into his body. He was tough, but he was still flesh and blood, and she couldn't understand why his wife had never insisted that he put away his uniform for good. One day ...

He nodded, reading her thoughts in her eyes. 'Sure, one day my luck will run out, but we've all got to go and I don't fancy growing old and weary and dependent. I've always looked out for myself and soldiering becomes a way of life and I'm too steeped in it—I guess like the leopard I can't change my spots.

'What about your wife, doesn't she count?' Eve asked, and it worried her that it was such an effort to mention his wife in a casual tone of voice. 'It can't be much of a life for her, surely?'

'It never was,' he said briefly. 'Do you like your coffee sweet?'

'Please.'

He dropped lumpy brown sugar in the big mug, poured the strong-looking coffee and handed it to her. 'There was one other reason why I didn't want you to go bathing in the creek,' he said. 'I'm not a spoilsport and I appreciate that a girl likes to be clean, but there could have been a leopard about and you wouldn't have seen him. Those lovely lithe creatures can almost flatten themselves to the ground and be invisible in the tall ferns, and if one of them leapt on you, you wouldn't stand any chance of getting away.'

'You're really laying the dangers on the line for me, aren't you, Major?' She sipped her coffee and gave him a challenging look. 'Do you reckon our chances of getting to Tanga are fairly good?'

'If you obey orders and don't treat the jungle as if it were a safari park, with big white hunters strolling about.'

Eve couldn't suppress a smile as she handed him the lion's share of the coffee, which was abominably strong. 'You have the edge of a *panga* to your tongue, Major O'Mara.'

'Do I scare you?' he jeered, taking a deep swig of the coffee. 'You surely guessed what you'd be in for when you decided to take this trek. I could have got you on that plane, you know. All I needed to do was sling that fat oaf out of his cushy seat.'

'Would you have preferred doing this trek with him?' she asked, looking demure.

Wade gave his lopsided smile. 'At least he wouldn't wander off in search of a bath, and lose his pants in the process.'

'Don't be mean.' Eve turned to the fire. 'Shall I dish up the sausage and beans?'

'No, I'd better do it. You might burn your dainty

67

little fingers and drop the lot in the flames.'

'You always have to be the *bwana*, don't you?'

'I have to be practical, *ndito*, and there's a difference. We haven't much food to see us through and it would be a pity to lose the dogs and beans.' As he spoke he whipped the can on to an enamel plate with the blade of his knife, and once again Eve had to admit to herself that he was very deft with his hard brown hands.

They ate hungrily and quickly, using biscuits to mop up the beans and sauce. The food was smoky, but somehow that added to the taste and Eve had never enjoyed a meal so much.

'I'll tidy up,' she said, when they had finished eating, anxious for him to go and look for her clothes.

'Right.' He stood up, flexing his arms. 'Leave the fire, lady. I'll see to that when I get back—that monkey swiped the garments from the creek bank, eh?'

'From the limb of one of those big mottled trees, just where the mud crabs appeared, then it darted back into the bush.'

'Well, keep your fingers crossed.' He loped off among the trees, and Eve set about tidying their camp site, wiping off the plates with handfuls of grass, folding the blanket after giving it a good shake and rolling it as tight as possible. All the while she was conscious of the jungle sounds all around her, and the tunnels of trees where anything might creep and be upon her before she could look around.

She tensed as she caught the rustling of leaves, but it was only one of the gorgeous sunbirds fluttering out on bright wings, pausing on a thick branch as if to watch her; and then it flew off again, its wings catching the sun that was now a flame of pure gold above the roof of towering trees.

Wade was at the edge of the clearing before she heard him, and then he called her name so he wouldn't alarm her. Relief caught at her heart that he was back, and with a quizzical look on his face he held out a couple of garments for her inspection. Her shirt, ripped and dirty, and her slacks with a piece of material hanging loose from the backside. 'No luck with the lingerie,' he said. 'I only hope your briefs aren't lying about on a bush somewhere, a sure indication that a woman has passed this way.'

'I took a spare pair from that woman's suitcase, so I can manage.' Eve ruefully examined the torn shirt. 'Lord, this is in a mess!'

'I expect a pair of monkeys were wrangling over it, until they got bored and went off in search of fresh mischief. I can't spare the time for any mending, Eve, so you'll have to make do——' He broke into a grin at the way she was regarding the backside of her slacks. 'We'll have to pin them, and then all you'll need is a dirty face to look like Judy Garland singing that tramp song with Astaire. Did you ever see that movie?'

'I can't somehow picture you as a film fan,' she said, watching him open a waterproof pouch in which he had cotton and needles, tablets and matches, a couple of candles, a tin of germicide plasters, and several large safety-pins attached to a piece of string.

'I was a member of the Green Jackets, not part of a holy order,' he handed her three of the safety pins. 'I went to the cinema when I had a couple of hours to spare, and contrary to popular belief it's a busy life in the army, especially if you belong to a regiment famous for its drilling and its marksmanship.'

'I'm glad you're a good shot, Major.' She accepted the pins and set about pinning her slacks into some sort of order. 'I imagine you are?'

'Sure.' He stroked a hand along the length of his Breda, almost as if it were part of a woman. 'This isn't army issue, but I found it some months ago in an abandoned plantation. It was probably used to hunt with, but these beauties can bring down a lion or an elephant.'

'I—I'm going to get dressed,' she said. 'Do you mind turning your back, Major?'

'Anything to oblige a lady.' He swung about as if on the parade ground, but not before she had seen his lips quirk at the edge. She felt the colour mount to the line of her hair, for when he had seen her in the altogether it must seem prudish to him that she hesitated to step into her slacks in front of him. The Major whistled that Garland-Astaire song as she scrambled into her garments—*We're a couple of swells, we live in the best hotels* . . .

'Are we really going to make it to Tanga today?' she asked, and was brushing at her dirty shirt when he turned to face her once more.

'All being well.' He slapped a hand against the mahogany grasp of his shotgun.

'Superstitious, Major?' It was her turn to smile.

'Soldiers are, lady. Have you never walked out on the arm of a dashing guardsman? I thought that was all part of the debutante set-up?'

'I've always preferred sailors,' she rejoined. 'My father was one.'

70

'A Naval Commander, no less?'

'No, he had a rather rakish yacht and he used to take Bahamian tourists out on fishing trips. One of the fools fell overboard on too much bourbon and my father was killed by a barracuda when he dived in to help his client.'

'That was a bad stroke of luck.' Wade O'Mara looked genuinely sympathetic. 'Is your mother still alive?'

Eve nodded and fingered a rent in her sleeve, poking her finger through it. 'She married a cotton-mill owner out in Peru. They have children of their own, so I was reared by my godfather. I—I owe him a lot, as you can imagine.'

'So it hasn't been all sugar and sunshine for you?'

'Is it ever? One would have to be a romantic optimist to ever believe that life can be like the movies, or one of those cloying novels you accused me of reading in bed. I actually prefer Raymond Chandler.'

'Well, that's one for the books.' He looked at her in a sort of pleased astonishment. 'I really rate that man! His atmosphere—Bogart, of course, was superb as Philip Marlowe. Well, what do you know! A gal who goes for the real thing in thrillers. Have you got a thing about James Bond?'

Eve shook her head, and thought how startlingly alive were his eyes in his unshaven face ... slithers of steel in much-worn leather. 'You sort of put me in mind of Bogart, do you know that?'

'*The African Queen*,' he drawled. 'Best movie ever made!'

'We seem to have something in common, then?'

'Anyway, let's hope we don't have to blow up an enemy battleship before we make it to Tanga.'

71

'I can't imagine the best hotel letting us in,' she smiled. 'We're hardly a pair of swells.'

She handed him his khaki shirt, but needless to say he didn't turn coyly away in order to put it on. He left it loose around his middle, but buttoned it to his throat. 'Just in case a mosquito fancies a piece of my hide,' he drawled.

'Put some of this on your neck and face.' Eve held out the tube of repellent.

He shook his head. 'That won't last much longer and you need it more than I do.' He came over and examined the rents in her shirt. 'Are your arms well smarmed with the stuff? Those little brutes go for tender meat.'

Eve nodded and could feel his fingers stroking against her arm through one of the rents, and for the briefest moment they stood like that in the jungle clearing, eyes meeting, senses suddenly alert to each other.

'I bet you look irresistible in tennis white,' he drawled, 'with one of those coloured bandeaux around your hair.'

Eve couldn't answer him in her usual quick way; she was so aware of him that her heart felt as if it were pounding in her throat. 'Afternoon tennis,' he went on, 'and then out to dine in a silver dress, with a fox fur like snow about your face. A far cry from all this, eh? And your escort a smooth-faced boy instead of a seasoned soldier trained to live by the gun and the *panga*.'

'No smooth-faced boy could get me to Tanga,' she said huskily. 'We'd better be on our way, hadn't we?'

'Right.' Wade released her arm, but where his hand had been Eve could feel her skin tingling ... electric sparks that seemed to be darting into her very veins.

72

Nothing like that had happened when James tentatively touched her ... never before had she felt such an awareness of another human being, and as she tied her bits and pieces into a plaid bundle, she was both sorry and glad that their trek to Tanga was almost over. There was a danger to this man that went beyond the fact that he was a tough mercenary soldier ... he made her aware of herself as a woman, and that was alarming, because always in the background of his life there hovered a wife and a son, and the last thing Eve wanted was to complicate her life by falling into an infatuation for a married man.

She had seen that happen to a couple of her friends, one of whom had become involved with a married man of fifty, and there had been a terrible scene when his wife found out what was going on. The wife had attempted suicide. and the girl had been discarded, to spend weeks feeling heart-stricken and used.

Eve recoiled from making that kind of mistake ... better to marry James than to fall for a man she could never call her own. The marriage would make her guardian happy, at least ... always supposing she could convince James that the mercenary Major had behaved like a perfect gentleman.

'What are you grinning about?'

She glanced somewhat guiltily at Wade ... then she realised that he was searching his pockets with a rather troubled frown meshing his eyebrows. He tapped each pocket in turn. then proceeded to turn them out, revealing a collection of oddments that included a gold medal on a grimy ribbon. Then he stuffed the things back in his pockets and began to look about on the ground.

'What have you lost?' Eve enquired, and for no good

reason she began to feel rather nervy.

'I can't find my compass,' he replied grimly.

'You mean—you've lost it?'

'Yes, dammit to hell. Must have happened when I went looking for your clothes, and the devil knows where it could have dropped out of my blasted pocket. I've gone and done what a raw recruit would have avoided unless he wanted a tongue-lashing!'

'You mean, Major, you need it in order to follow the trail correctly? That we might get lost if——'

He pressed his lips into a grim line and thumbed his jaw, rasping the black bristles. 'I should have made sure the compass was safely lodged in my pocket, and now it's lying somewhere in the jungle and I either lose more time searching for it, or we take a chance and plough on and hope to God we don't lose ourselves.'

'Do you feel you ought to search for the compass?' she asked worriedly.

He glanced at his watch. 'Every hour we spend in this part of the territory is ripe with danger. I'd like to chance our arm, if you're game, Eve?'

She gazed at his strong, irregular features ... unyielding and unafraid. It was a face that gave her courage; in fact she was prepared to bet that he had chanced his arm on more than one occasion and had beaten the odds.

'Let's take a chance and go on,' she said. She glanced about her at the tangled jungle, thirsting under the hot sun, with vapour beginning to rise around them. Suddenly the place took on a menace that made her want to be on the move. 'You know the risks better than I, and it does feel risky to remain here any longer.'

'Either way it's a risky decision, Eve. I'll be honest

with you, I could lead you astray.'

She met his grey eyes, slivers of pure steel in his hard brown face. 'I've trusted your judgment so far, haven't I?'

'You have, lady, but don't burst into tears if we end up in the midle of nowhere instead of the airport at Tanga.' Having said that he began to stamp out the fire, brushing big leaves over the ground where it had been, and tossing deep among the big ferns the stones he had used for a stove.

'*C'est la vie*,' he murmured. 'I heard a guy say that in a film once—was it Alan Ladd?—and it sounds exactly right for this occasion.'

'What will be, will be,' she said, hoisting her bundle.

'Right. And if we do lose ourselves, the golden rule is —stay calm. Think you will, lady?'

'Hope I will.' She brought a smile to her lips, but remembering it was her fault that the precious compass was lost, her smile melted swiftly away. 'I'm sorry, Major.'

'Regret is a waste of time, and we've wasted enough of that. All set, and quite comfortable. The sandals okay, and the ankle?'

He had brought her sandals back with him from the creek bank where she had left them, and as she nodded, hope ignited in her eyes. 'We could search along by the creek, couldn't we?'

'We're going to, so keep your fingers crossed.'

Eve would have crossed all ten toes and fingers if it would have helped, but unfortunately there was no glinting betrayal of the compass in the mounds of rank vegetation, alive with horrible-looking crabs that scuttled away from the kicking movements of Wade's boots.

Finally he gritted his teeth and gave a resigned shrug. 'We can't waste any more time, so let's be moving along. Got your walking stick?'

She nodded and off they set along a path that had to be cleared every step of the way by a hefty swing of the *panga* in Wade's hand, lopping the rubbery leaves and spiny branches with an ease that formed in Eve's mind a mental image of what that kind of blade could do to human flesh.

It was like walking in a monotonous dream, for everything had a sameness to it ... the same tangles of trailing vines, curtains of dank moss and fern, plaitings of whiplike tree-limbs. The smells alone had some kind of variation, musky from the clumps of orchids, earthy and almost sinister when they struck a patch of rotted vegetation, almost seductively scented by velvety bells big enough to hide a snake.

Eve could feel the sweat running down her spine, her thighs, and the slight valley between her breasts. There were innumerable flies, gnats and other venomous things flying about in the stripings of sunlight, but she followed on doggedly, blinking her sweat-clustered lashes and wincing at the soreness this produced after a while.

When they paused for a five-minute rest, Wade handed her a few more berries, big as strawberries, squashy and tasteless, but they helped to moisten her mouth and throat.

'We could have boiled some of that creek water, except that even a boiling might not have killed off some of the tougher germs that breed where decay is rampant. We don't want cholera, eh?'

'God, no!'

'We might come across some coconut palms, and if the nuts are green we'll have ourselves something to drink, but in the meantime I'm preserving what we have left in the water bottle.'

'I bet you wish I was a boy,' she said, licking the last remnant of juice from her lips. 'Then you wouldn't concern yourself quite so much, would you?'

'Who says I'm concerned about you?' he jeered.

Eve flushed slightly and evaded his eyes, which could look so mocking when he liked. 'I don't think you're quite as hard-boiled as you make out.'

'Don't kid yourself, lady. In my kind of army you have to be tough in order to survive, and I'd be tough on whoever I had with me—even a creamy-skinned little vixen from the manor.'

'Is the sarcasm meant to pepper me up?' she asked, and beneath her shirt her creamy skin felt as if a flame had swept over it.

'What do you reckon?'

She dared to look at him, but his face was imperturbable and her vision was too sweat-blurred to take an accurate reading. 'I shouldn't imagine that anyone has ever got into your mind and found out what you're really thinking,' she said. 'I bet you're an awfully good poker player, aren't you?'

'You wouldn't lose your bet,' he drawled. 'Shall we make tracks, *ndito*?'

'Ready when you are, *bwana*.'

'Attagirl!'

CHAPTER FIVE

It was well into the afternoon when they reached the deserted village, a settlement of huts within a broken-down sapling fence, where the foliage was much trampled, as if a number of people had passed this way.

Eve was cautioned to remain among the trees while the Major, shotgun at the ready, went into the compound and made a search of the huts, most of them having been destroyed by fire so that only the palmwood supports remained.

It was at a bend of the clearing that one of the huts stood in dilapidated isolation, with its dark mud-constructed walls and roof thatching still intact. When Wade returned to where Eve was waiting he briskly informed her that the village was quite benighted, as if everyone had fled away from a sudden attack, which had probably taken place at least a month ago.

'One of the huts is in fair condition, so we're going to rest there,' he said, shooting his cuff and taking a look at his watch. 'We've walked far enough and it will soon grow dark.'

'We're lost, aren't we?' she said carefully. She didn't want to sound as if she were blaming him, not when most of the fault weighed on her conscience. 'It's all right, I'm not going to have hysterics, but I would prefer to be told the truth.'

'Hopelessly lost,' he confessed. 'These jungle trails are all so much alike without a map or a compass, and we probably branched off unaware some miles back.

It's a good thing the village is deserted—you can't always be sure if the people are rebel sympathisers, and it would appear from the state of this settlement that the people were burned out and chased off into he bush.'

'They weren't killed?' she asked, looking about her and seeing the thickening of the shadows, and hearing the rising crescendo of bird calls and the thrashing sound of monkeys moving high in the trees. A parakeet squawked and her nerves crawled.

Wade shook his head. 'They may have been driven off by mercenaries, but there's no sign of any kind of slaughter. They may even have burned the huts themselves and gone off in search of a safer location. Anyway, we'll take a chance and sleep beneath a roof tonight. Come along, Eve, let's try and make ourselves comfortable.'

'C'est la vie,' she smiled shakily, and followed him across the compound on sore and aching feet. How she would have loved to plunge her poor feet into a bowl of water into which a handful of seaweedy salts had been scattered, but instead she had to stand on them in the doorway of a smelly hut while Wade directed his torch around the curving walls. She had to force herself not to cry out when something scuttled across the floor and a heavy army boot crushed the thing to atoms.

'I—I think I'd prefer to sleep in the open,' she said. 'This place isn't exactly cosy, is it?'

'The trouble is, Eve, I think it's going to rain. I felt a few spots as we crossed the compound and when it rains out here it means business and we'd be soaked to the skin in a matter of minutes. Better to rest here for the night.'

'So long as we can have some light.' Eve shivered and

peered into the dark corners of the hut, her nostrils tensing at the smell of smoke, dried mud and rotting leaves that pervaded the place. Wade had dumped his knapsack on the floor and was investigating various objects which had been left behind in the evacuation of the village ... some abandoned spears with lethal-looking tips, a gourd which emitted a liquid sound when shaken, a wicker fishing-basket, and some large fire stones. Wade examined the fishing-basket with a keen, glinting look in his eyes.

'It could be that we aren't far from a running stream,' he remarked. 'If so, Eve, we may get ourselves some fish for breakfast.'

'That will be nice,' she smiled at the prospect of running water rather than the food. She watched as he took the stopper out of the gourd and put the open top to his nostrils, taking a deep sniff at the contents.

'Honey-beer—intoxicating as the very devil!'

'Are you going to drink it?' she asked.

'Not on your life, lady. I don't fancy a day-long hangover. A long cool Lion beer is more my mark.'

'Thank goodness for that!' The prospect of camping in this mud hut was bad enough but Eve had momentarily quailed at the image of a drunken soldier sharing it with her.

He shot her a quizzical look. 'Getting drunk isn't one of my vices,' he assured her. 'I like to gamble now and again, and love nothing better than a keen day at the races, but I've never seen much sense in getting a thick head, and a beery pot-belly.'

She smiled and ran her eyes down the lean length of him—formidable, and packed with the strength and will to survive against very long odds. They were lost in the jungle, but for tonight he'd make the most of this ramshackle dwelling of thatch and hardened mud, its roof woven from big leaves matted over bamboo lathes. Wade's aura certainly wasn't tranquil, but to Eve's eyes he was a bulwark between her and all those hazards that took on a nightmare quality as the darkness crept over the surrounding jungle. He was so sure and capable, and she took hope from the very look of him, especially when he emptied the gourd of beer into the tall shaggy grass outside the hut and remarked that if they were lucky enough to be close to a stream, the gourd could be used for water.

'Nothing ever throws you off balance, does it, Major?'

'You think not?' His eyes quizzed her in the deepening dusk light. 'Just as well to go on thinking it, lady. I wouldn't want to disillusion you.'

'It isn't fair to harbour too many illusions about people,' she said.

'A wise remark which you probably culled from a Shaw play, for he was quite a cynical old guy in his way.'

'It isn't cynicism, it's sense.' Eve tilted her chin. 'I can't imagine that you harbour any illusions about— women.'

'You'd be surprised, honey.'

Her skin warmed at the way he almost purred that word. It would have been wiser to discontinue the conversation, but she couldn't fight the curiosity which he aroused in her ... in that side of him that wasn't all soldier.

'Even you, Major?'

'Even I, so try not to shatter my illusions.'

'They must be very fragile?'.

'Spun-glass.' He had unstrapped his knapsack and taken from it the waterproof pouch in which he kept his matches and candles. He lit one and held it so the shadows played over his face, giving him a rather devilish look. 'I wonder if in normal circumstances we'd talk like this, eh? Right now you'd probably be getting ready for a date at the Ritz Grill or the White House restaurant, slipping your slim legs into sheer hose, worried about what to wear instead of looking like a weary, worn doll I've pushed to the very edge of exhaustion. Yet you stand up to me, don't you, lady? You back-answer me, instead of scratching my eyes out for getting you lost in this neck of the woods. Where did you learn to be so gritty?'

'I—I went to a good finishing school,' she said, being flippant because it didn't do to let anything he said get too embedded in her emotions.

'It could have been Sandhurst from the way you're taking all this,' he quipped. 'They'd have presented you with a jewelled Sword of Honour. I think you get it from your father, eh?'

She nodded. 'I very much hope so—as your son probably gets his drive from you.'

'Aren't we being nice to each other?' he mocked. 'D'you reckon this was the local courting hut?'

'I—I hope not.' She backed away from him, and immediately he broke into a gruff laugh.

'Ease up, little one. I'm just damn glad that you aren't a dumb bunny, for amusing as they are, it would be hell right now to be stuck with a gal like that.'

'I thought men liked the dumb and compliant type of female?'

'It's a myth, Eve. Men like common sense, especially in a tight spot. That's how Mr. Churchill won his war —the women held on and didn't panic, even when the roof caved in and they went on knitting socks under the kitchen table. Quite a people, the Cockneys.'

'They're your people, aren't they?' she said.

'On my mother's side. She worked a vegetable barrow on the sunny side of the Chapel Street market in Islington. Tall, vital brunette, with plenty of nerve and lots of friendly chat. Went and married a nogood Irishman with too much charm, who ran out on her and left her with me to bring up. She did okay, until she caught a bad chill one winter day and never recovered from it. I was nine years old and placed in a State home, which is not to be confused with a stately one, and needless to say when the time came I took to the army like a stray duck taking to a millpond. It's all I've ever known —for a good long time, anyway.'

'What about—I mean, there's your wife.' It dismayed Eve that she always seemed to trip over her tongue whenever she mentioned his wife.

'Sure, but married quarters aren't bad,' he drawled. Soldiers move around a lot, especially ambitious ones who want stripes, and then crowns on the shoulder.'

'Did she never mind your way of life?' Eve asked tentatively.

'Mind?' There was a crystal hardness to his voice. When a woman marries a serving man she had to accept his way of life—it's as simple as that.'

It sounded uncompromising and far from tender, and Eve saw the adamant set to his jaw as he went across the hut and affixed the candle to one of the fire stones, so that the flame was out of the draught of the doorway.

'Let's get ourselves settled,' he said curtly. 'I'd better get some water boiled for our tea before the rain comes down. You lay out the blanket and take a look at those few cans of food we've got left. I believe one of them has pork and ham in it, and we might as well make a fuss of ourselves—I meant to have got you to Tanga, damn careless fool that I am!'

'No, you can't take all the blame, Wade.' Eve caught at his arm before she could prevent herself and there in the flickering shadows cast by the candle they looked at each other ... she could feel the tension biting into him, and a dark groove had fixed itself between his eyebrows. 'I disobeyed an order of yours, Major, and that's why we're in this predicament. I bet I'd be in the glasshouse if this were our barracks.'

He smiled briefly. 'Female discipline bears no relation to the masculine sort. I can't expect you to think and react like a recruit being trained for the regiment —you're far too female for that.'

'All the same, I bet you'd like to give me a good hard shake.'

'Sure,' he agreed, 'until your milk teeth rattle. But what a good thing for you I've had a kid of my own and know how mettlesome the young can be—you'd like him, Eve. He's a good-looking young pup—takes after my mother for his looks.'

'Oh, I'd have said——' She broke off almost shudderingly, seeing beneath the dark stubble, the sun-lined skin, the erosion of his own youth, a face that made her heart give a jolt. She felt as if she had just saved herself on the edge of a precipice, and she moved back carefully away from that precipitous edge and bent over his knapsack, taking a deep breath of recovery as she took out the army blanket and began to unwind it.

Eve was glad when he went outside and began to gather wood for a fire. Oh lord, how easy for someone inexperienced to suddenly feel the potent, overpowering charm of a man so much older, who had seen and done things she could only guess at. He had killed, made love, known what it was like to have a child of his own placed in his arms. Eve saw the need to fight against the attraction he had for her, but how was she going to manage it, thrown together as they had been, in the primitive heart of the African jungle?

She flattened the blanket out carefully on the floor she wished she could have swept and scrubbed. There were webs up there in the bamboo lathes of the ceiling, and she knew there were things crawling about in the dark corners of the hut. With resolution she shut her mind to them and set about laying out biscuits on the plates and opening the tin of pork and ham. It smelled good and she felt her stomach react hungrily, but until Wade brought in the tea she left the meat in the tin and fitted the lid back on, just in case a fly or a crawly came to investigate that delicious aroma.

She went again to the knapsack, for in her exploration she had come upon Wade's shaving-mirror and was curious to see how she looked after a day of scrambling about in the jungle. A scarecrow, that was the only word that adequately described her appearance. Dark red hair tangled, a scratch on her forehead where a branch had whipped at her, eyes enormous and filled with a hundred uncertain questions. As for her clothes —they were just about fit for the rag-bag! Oh well, it couldn't be helped, but she had to make her hair a bit tidier before sitting down to supper.

Untying her plaid bundle, she found the comb, a good tortoiseshell one, thank goodness, and began to tug it vigorously through the sweat-knotted tangles ... the days of luxury shampoos in a Bond Street salon seemed a thousand moons ago. There she had sat, an idle, smartly clad, bored young debutante, glancing through a magazine and swinging a well-shod foot ... undreaming that one dusky night she would find herself sharing a primitive mud hut with a black-haired mercenary twenty years her senior, who wouldn't hesitate to put a bullet through her head if they were fallen upon by bloodthirsty rebels.

Eve stared into her bundle and her fingers closed on the expensive crystal atomiser she had been unable to resist, though Wade had told her not to lumber herself with anything that wasn't necessary. But then Major O'Mara most definitely wasn't a woman!

With a tiny smile she squeezed the atomiser and felt the perfume cool and fragrant against her skin ... mmmm, that was lovely, irresistible, a breath of civilisation in the midst of the untamed. Feeling a little tidier, she went outside the hut to see how Wade was coping. The kettle was bubbling away on the homemade hob, but Wade was nowhere in sight and Eve felt a clutch of alarm, her own hand pressing itself to her throat.

What an idiot she was! No one would carry Wade off without one hell of a struggle, so he had probably gone scouting for more wood, and was checking to see that it was safe to camp here for the night. The rain was coming down a little harder now, hitting against the hot fire stones and making them sizzle. The rain was welcome against Eve's skin, and way up there in the density of the sky she could see unbelievable groupings of stars. When the rain increased they would be blotted out, but for the moment she could enjoy their beauty ... she tensed as she caught the sound of someone moving in the bush that crowded to the back of the hut.

'Wade?'

No deep voice answered her, and Eve felt a prickling of her scalp, a sensation of fear like cold bony fingers creeping down her spine. She also smelled an aroma that blotted out the *Tabu* perfume she had sprayed on herself ... it was a powerful smell of an alley where cats had freely roamed. It wafted towards Eve and she felt herself gagging, she prepared to flee into the hut ...

'Don't make a single move!'

Wade's voice was so soft it was almost a whisper, but there was a command in it which she instantly obeyed, freezing into stillness as his tall figure advanced across the compound, with the Breda in a firing position.

Then the rustling sound came again and the next instant that strong ammoniac smell was gone, and Wade was between Eve and whatever lurked in the bush.

'A female leopard on the hunt,' he said quietly. 'I'm glad you had the nerve to stand perfectly still. Those creatures react very swiftly, and mostly out of fear of the unknown. Your scent was probably as acute to that cat as hers was to you.'

'Thanks,' Eve said shakily. 'I hope I don't smell like a back alley where all the cats have been prowling.'

He laughed in his brief way and lowered the Breda. Then he suddenly leaned close to her and sniffed at her hair. 'That isn't cat—smells more like the perfume counter at Woolworths.'

'It covers up some of the sweat,' she said defensively.

'Putting on perfume in the jungle!' he jeered. 'Is it for my benefit?'

'No, it isn't! My morale needed a boost.'

'What's it called? *Seduction*?'

'No!' She moved sharply away from his taunting tallness, and went to pass him, only to be blocked by his suddenly flung out arm.

'Scents usually have names, don't they? Put me wise.'

'It's called *Tabu*, if you must know. Now let's have supper.'

'Tabu, as in don't touch or the gods will send down thunder?'

'It's raining harder and we're both getting wet— and I'm hungry.'

'Don't try anything on with me, Eve, for this is no garden of Eden we're alone in.' He grated the words. 'We're both made of human stuff, but we've got to keep this strictly on a rescue operations level so that there'll be no regrets on your side or mine when, and if, you make it home to the boy-friend. Understand me?'

'I—I wasn't even thinking about you when I applied the perfume.' She was shocked by what he had said, and then she felt her temper flare and she had to say things that would hurt him if possible, the way he had hurt her, turning something innocent into the act of a wanton. 'As you've pointed out, Major O'Mara, you're old enough to be my father, and I'd want my head tested if I started throwing myself at you! Sweaty, unshaven, with the brutal tongue of a trooper!

I should hope I was a bit more fastidious, thank you!'

'That's more like it, girl. You keep on hating my guts and we'll get along just fine.' He gave her a slight push towards the hut, for the rain was whipping at them, plastering their hair into wet jags and running in drops down their faces.

'Don't shove me!' Her eyes flamed into his. 'Chauvinistic brute!'

'Right, if you want to get wet, that's your lookout.' He swung the kettle off the fire and went inside with it, leaving her to stand fuming in the rain hungry for her supper, but mortified by his assumption that she had scented herself like a tart in order to arouse his sensual feelings. Oh, damn and blast him, why hadn't she let him make room for her on the plane forcibly, so that she could have flown to Tanga with the nuns? Now she was benighted with him in the middle of a jungle, and she had to endure the rough edge of his tongue, and his insults.

Eve blinked the rain off her lashes and felt her shirt clinging to her shoulders ... letting herself get soaked like this was ridiculous, and she marched into the hut, where an aroma of strong tea mingled with the smell of the pork and ham, which she had sliced and laid on the plates.

'We don't have to quarrel.' He indicated that she sit down on the blanket. 'Come on, where's your smile?'

'Seems like I've lost it,' she rejoined, and she sat down as far away as possible from his lounging figure.

'I hope you haven't lost your appetite.' Wade held out her plate and she accepted it with a mutter of thanks. They settled down to eat and drink, while the rain hissed on the thatch roof above them, and the trees thrashed and whined in the rising wind outside in the wet night.

'A bit of luck finding this rondavel,' he drawled. 'It wouldn't have been pleasant having to spend a night in the rain. I have a packet of fruit and nuts if you'd like some?'

'No, thanks.' She gazed across the hut away from him. 'I've had all I want.'

'Sulky females are a pain in the neck.' He lounged back on his elbow and picked biscuit crumbs off the blanket. 'I can't make you out. Surely you're woman enough to know that this isn't exactly the place or the time to try a bit of teasing? I might be a lot older than you, but I'm still capable.'

'I'm sure you are,' she said coldly. 'But it never entered my head to tease you—I felt scruffy and sticky and scent's a good cover up. They used it enough in the old days, when bathing wasn't all that popular.'

Eve still wouldn't look at him, but she could feel his eyes upon her profile, intent and steely.

'Is it possible you're so innocent?' he drawled.

She scorned to answer him, tilting her nose and giving her attention to the persistent sound of the rain. Suddenly she shivered and without comment he arose and placed across the doorway the rather battered leaf-woven screen meant for that purpose. It was primitive but it served, shutting out most of the draught that had been blowing in. The hut had been stuffy at first, but now Eve was glad that the cold had been blocked out.

'That better?' he asked, starting to roll himself a cigarette, the shadows made by the candle flickering over his lean face and making his bones seem harshly defined. In order to save a match he bent to the candle flame and lit his cigarette, and Eve resented his air of being at no one's beck and call, least of all a woman's. But she had to accept his orders, and his sardonic reprimands ... even those she hadn't earned.

'The real trouble with you,' he said, 'is that you're tired and edgy and just a bit scared.'

'Not of you,' she assured him, and watching his keen enjoyment of his after-supper smoke she wished she had accepted his offer of a few nuts and raisins. She curled down on the blanket with her head at rest on her plaid bundle, feeling herself go taut when Wade came and stood over her.

'No, not of me, you've too much spirit for that.' He gestured towards the doorway and ash fell from his cigarette. 'It's all that jungle out there, and how we're going to find our way out of it. Look, I'm going to make a suggestion that you may not care for, but I think it's a good one. I believe we're fairly close to a stream or even a river—now listen, every now and again you hear a tree crash in the rain, don't you?'

She nodded and wondered why his suggestion, when it came, wasn't going to appeal to her ... was it going to be so awful? Was he going to leave her here and go off on his own to look for a way out?

'I—I know I hold you up in these sandals,' Eve was up on her knees and her eyes were pleading with him, 'but don't leave me here, please! I'd be terrified——'

'What are you talking about?' He leant down and took her by the chin, his eyes searching her scared face. 'Leave you here—no, you've got it all wrong, lady. Those trees you hear falling are coming loose from the

91

soil, their roots being the sort that travel along the ground instead of under it, and some of those trees are all but hollow. If we're near a river, then I'm suggesting that I build us a boat and we continue our journey by water. We're bound to land up——'

'A boat?'

'A canoe.' He knelt down facing her and his eyes were eager. 'I have the *panga* and the blade is a good sharp one, so I should have no problem shaping out a canoe and making a paddle. It will be better on the water than slogging through the jungle, and there's always a food supply on hand in the shape of fish. The only problem is that it would probably take me about a week to tackle the job, and we'd have to stay here in the rondavel—take a chance on it.'

Eve stared at him and could feel her heart pounding. 'You're serious, aren't you?' she said.

He nodded. 'To be quite frank with you, lady, I don't think you'd last out very much longer in the jungle. When your repellent runs out, you'll be bitten unmercifully, and in those sandals your feet will soon be wrecked. If I take the time to make us a canoe, you can ride on the water, you can eat fish and keep up your mineral strength—fish is a marvellous food, probably the best, even catfish, who look as ugly as sin but make darn good cod-like steaks, baked over a fire. Well, what do you say? Are you with me?'

'Have I a choice?'

He smiled at the edge of his mouth and had a look of cool-eyed recklessness. 'Not really, Eve. For your own sake you've got to fall in with my idea.'

'Even though it will be risky to stay on here?' she asked.

'Even so.'

Eve let her gaze rest on his hard, determined jaw. She felt his vigorous strength of will ... his ability to survive against alarming odds. He was right about her, a few more days like today in the jungle and she'd keel over, a bundle of helpless misery he might just manage to carry on his back for a while.

'All this depends on whether we're near a river,' she said. 'What if we aren't?'

'Then we have no choice but to trek on.'

'Then let's keep our fingers crossed, Major.'

He nodded and for a moment his teeth were bared in a half-savage smile. 'If they taught you prayer at that mission, then say a prayer tonight, before you drop off to sleep. Say a couple, one for each of us.'

'Don't you ever pray?' she asked.

'Me?' He ground the stub of his cigarette into one of the empty plates. 'The angels don't listen to wicked men like me, lady.' And it was as he spoke that a resounding clap of thunder shook the hut, and shook loose something from the overhead lathes. It fell near Eve and ran across her legs, trailing a long thin tail. She shrieked and cowered away, while Wade leapt in pursuit of the rodent, swinging aside the woven screen so the palm rat was able to streak out into the pelting rain, lit by vivid flashes of lightning that illuminated the tall shapes of the trees.

'Oh God!' Eve flung her hands over her face, not so much from fear of the rat but from her own terrified reaction. She had never been one of those females who swooned at the sight of rats, bats or mice, for she had been brought up in the country, and the stables and attics of her guardian's house were harbours for all sorts of things that crept and crawled and went bump in the night—Lake House was even supposed to have its own ghost—but just now she had felt her nerves give way and it had frightened her.

She couldn't stop shaking, and abruptly Wade pulled her against him and pressed her head to his shoulder. 'I know, kid,' he murmured, 'you're having a rough time for the first time in your life, but you're doing fine, believe me. Rats aren't pretty, but they're less dangerous than the two-legged variety of *bête noire*.'

'I—I'm not usually so jumpy, a—and I've seen rats before,' she said raggedly. 'You must think me an awful baby.'

'I think you what you are, a young girl caught up in a tricky situation you've never had to face before.' He held her and rocked her a little, and right through her shirt Eve could feel the hard warmth of his hand.

'I think I'd go crazy if you weren't here with me,' she said, then she jumped again as there came another loud peal of thunder followed by the nerve-wrenching crash as a large tree suddenly lost its grip in the mud and keeled over ... like a felled giant.

'Want to try a jigger of whisky?' he asked. 'I've a small flask of it and I've been saving it for an emergency.'

'But this isn't an emergency, Major. I'm just being —childish.'

'Well, I fancy a snort, and I insist you join me.' He let her go, giving her shoulder a reassuring pat ... being fatherly, she told herself, even though she felt reactions to his touch that were not those of a daughter.

'I never realised that the jungle could be so—so fearful.' She crouched there with her arms about herself, while incessant peals of thunder rumbled around the hut, and a cataract of rain drummed down on the roof. Lightning ripped like claws at their doorway and through the chinks she saw a reddish flare as a tree or a bush was struck, breaking into flame that was just as quickly smothered by the downpour.

'The jungle's very much alive, Eve.' He unscrewed the flask and measured the spirit into the tea mug. 'Anything alive can cause fear, anguish and alarm—here, drink this and let it settle your nerves.'

She accepted the mug and took a tentative sip at the whisky. It was strong and she had never cared for the taste, but she knew it would help her get rid of the shakes. He nodded and gave her an intent look when she handed him the empty mug. 'It's smoothing out the creases already, eh?'

Eve nodded and watched him toss back his own measure of whisky. His black hair looked as if it hadn't seen a comb for days, and his unshaven jaw gave him the look of a convict on the run. Eve suddenly laughed and couldn't stop herself.

'That's better,' he drawled. 'I can deal with the giggles, but a woman's tears are something else.'

'You wouldn't be so amused if you knew what I was thinking,' she said.

'You're dying to tell me, so why not indulge yourself?'

'You look a fearful roughneck, Major O'Mara. I'm wondering what you look like when you've had a shave.'

'I may give you that pleasure in the morning, young Eve.' He replaced his flask in the knapsack and began to brush out the blanket so they could settle down for the night. 'Tomorrow, all being well, we'll take a look around our *zona inexplorada* and see what it has to offer.'

He gnawed a moment on his lip with his firm teeth. 'Let's hope I'm right about that river—I've got a feeling I am, for it isn't unusual to find a native settlement within reach of one. Offer up a small prayer to *Ngai*, just to be on the safe side.'

He rolled the mosquito netting around her, for suddenly she had grown very sleepy and was drowsily aware of him leaning over her for a moment. 'Sleep deep and forget everything,' he advised. 'Make pretend you're in your flounced fourposter at the family mansion.'

'I'd really need a vivid imagination for that.' She smiled, the lids of her eyes weighted with exhaustion. 'I never even shared my fourposter with a replica of Humphrey Bogart, though I thought about it after seeing *Casablanca*.'

The white teeth glimmered above her in the dark face, and already half-asleep, she wasn't certain if he brushed at the tumbled hair on her temples.

CHAPTER SIX

WHEN Eve crawled out of her warm nest of plaid robe and netting, she saw that the hut was empty and was about to panic when she breathed a drift of woodsmoke and realised that Wade was just outside, probably getting breakfast. Yawning and stretching, she wandered out into the hazy morning sunlight, to find the kettle on the fire, and Wade busily lathering his chin. He had attached his shaving-mirror to a branch and was stripped of his shirt, his trousers belted against his firm brown body.

Eve caught the scrape of the blade through the strong growth of beard and she had a feeling he was watching her through the mirror.

'You had a good night,' he said. 'Slept sound as an infant in its cot, even though the thunder kept on for quite a while.'

'I do feel rested,' she said, and glanced about the compound, where moisture was still dripping from the surrounding trees. Over everything there hung the scent of wet foliage, and there was a busy chattering and whistling in the bush. 'What are we having for breakfast?'

'How about smoky bacon, with eggs and toast?' he drawled.

'Don't torture me,' she groaned. 'It looks as if we'll have to make do with smoky beans straight from the can.'

'Eve,' he turned to face her with half his face shaven clean, 'aren't you curious that we have water in the kettle? Last night the water-bottle was empty, this morning it's full.'

'You mean——?'

He nodded, the sun on the warm coppery gleam of his skin. Eve felt a sudden tumult of her pulses, an awareness of her own scarecrow appearance.

'A river,' she breathed. 'That means we can bathe and catch fish and be a little civilised!'

'Later on,' he agreed. 'But right after breakfast I want to explore the village for any useful implements, and I want to take a look at the trees around here. There's also the chance that when the villagers ran off they left behind them a few vegetables in their patches of cultivated ground. Can you see to the tea while I finish off my face?'

'Yes, *bwana*.' Eve was suddenly optimistic, and she liked the feel of the sunlight on her face as she set about making breakfast for them. Wade was tough and tantalising, and he could be diamond-hard when he chose but given half a chance he'd make that boat and they'd get away on the water without having to take their chance in the jungle. She felt like singing, and compromised by whistling to herself as she opened the beans, replaced the lift halfway and set the can carefully on the fire stones.

This wasn't such a bad place to camp in for a while, not if she kept her mind firmly closed to images of wild-eyed rebels through the bush, coming so suddenly that Wade didn't have time to reach for his Breda. She shot him a look and saw that he was wiping the soap from his face; the shotgun was close at hand, leaning against the tree on which his mirror was suspended.

She felt reassured, and then he turned to look at her and as their eyes met across the clearing Eve felt a sudden weakness in her limbs. It was the first time she had seen him clean-shaven and for a moment he was a stranger, the roughneck replaced by a man of lean distinction, who in full officer's uniform would look ... dashingly attractive.

Suddenly she felt rather shy of him and could feel an irregularity in her breathing as he swung his Breda on to his bare coppery shoulder and began to stroll across to her. Clad only in his khaki trousers there was a supple rippling of hard muscle under the sun-darkened skin, and Eve felt a stab of physical reaction that made her clench her teeth. She hadn't known that awareness of a man could be so potent, like a heady gulp of wine followed by an alarming mixture of weakness and elation; added to which was the scared feeling that he was going to guess how she felt.

With an effort of will she managed to sound insouciant. 'Tea's up, and the beans are smoking, and do take a look at those little gold-breasted birds flying about. Are they canaries?'

'Probably a wild species.' He rested the shotgun and gazed down at her, his lip quirking. 'Well, do you think I look a trifle more civilised now my bristles are gone?'

'Don't tantalise me with your manly beauty,' she said demurely. 'This isn't the garden of Eden we're lost in.'

'*Touché.*' There was a grating amusement in his drawl. 'Glad to see you're back on form and aren't letting this situation get you down.'

'Sunshine and bird-calls, and hot sweet tea, can do

wonders for the morale, Major. I'm making believe I'm on a camping trip with the local scoutmaster.'

He caught her gaze and made an intent search of her eyes, then he added approvingly, 'I wouldn't have taken much of a bet on a high-society gal making much of a companion in adversity, but you're proving me wrong, aren't you?'

'So far,' she said, handing him his share of the tea. 'Last night I lost a good mark, but the rat took me by surprise. Normally I don't squeal like that, and I've seen plenty of rats and bats at Lake House.'

'The guardian's country seat, I take it?'

'Yes, in Essex. I've boated on the lake, so I should be able to do my share of the paddling when you get the canoe ready for launching.'

'On the smooth waters, perhaps.' He leaned down to slide the can of beans off the fire. 'But some of these rivers run into rapids—we'll wait and see how things go. Take care with this sauce, it's hot.'

They tucked into their beans and only had a couple of biscuits each, for they were fast running out of them and they had to substitute for a longed-for slice of bread.

He had brought back enough water for Eve to be able to wash her face and hands, after which she applied the hateful repellent. Wade washed his shirt in the one-legged iron pot and hung it on a bush to dry in the sun. 'Let's hope a monkey doesn't run off with it,' he said, and they stood a moment watching the agile chimps flinging themselves about in the high trees, chattering and showing their teeth to the pair of human beings. Suddenly something bounced down hard near Wade's feet, and he bent to pick up the object. It was a large coconut!

100

'Manna from the monkeys,' Wade said delightedly. He shook the nut and the liquid inside swished about. 'Well, if we can find a few more of these, we'll have coconut meat and milk to supplement our diet. Fancy a piece right now?'

'No, I'll have some later on, but you go ahead.'

'No, I'll wait as well. I'm eager to have a look round this place and do some scavenging.' He went into the hut and put the nut away with their dwindling supplies of food, and then together they searched the ruins of the other huts but found nothing that was still usable, but they were lucky enough to find some patches of cultivation where upon scraping with his hands Wade unearthed several large, knobbly-looking yams, some wild spinach, and cobs of corn.

They were congratulating themselves on this little crock of eatables, when to their astonishment they heard a gobbling sound from among the bushes and the next instant a turkey came pecking its way into the yard where they were standing. It cocked an eye at them, and then went on thrusting its yellow beak in and out of the dirt, where there must have been some stray corn seed.

Wade caught Eve's glance and his eyes cautioned her not to move and startle the bird, which despite its rather scrawny appearance could provide them with a couple of square meals. Eve wasn't chicken-hearted, but she had never been right on the scene when a bird for the table had had its neck wrung, but she knew from the look on Wade's face that he was about to do just that the instant he got his hands on the turkey.

He leapt, there was a wild squawk, a flutter of feathers, and Eve turned away as the powerful hands did their work. Why would he hesitate? She had to remember all the time that Wade had killed men just as easily and efficiently; that he had given himself to warfare as a monk to religion.

'You can open your eyes,' he drawled. 'And think of it like this, if I'm going to build a boat I need to have my strength built up.'

'It's just that a minute ago the poor thing was pecking away without a care in the world, and now——'

Now the limp body hung from Wade's hand and there wasn't even the remotest look of compunction in the steel-grey eyes that met Eve's.

'We have to eat,' he said curtly. 'There isn't a supermarket round the corner where the frozen poultry is stacked in its container, having come from the battery farm where those poor things never get a chance to peck about in a yard. You'll enjoy your drumstick as much as I shall, along with baked beans and some of these greens. A solid meal will do wonders for both of us.'

'I know that, but you're so——'

'Is ruthless the word you're searching for, Eve?'

'Not quite, but you are unmercifully efficient when it comes to the crunch, aren't you?'

'I've had to be, lady. In Malaya, Cyprus, Belfast—and out here. He who hesitates is a goner. Now let's take this helpful hoard of food to the hut and then we'll take a look at some of those trees that fell in the storm last night.'

'Can't you take me to the river while you have a look round in the jungle?' she asked, carrying greens and corncobs in her arms as they made their way back to the hut. 'It will be cooler there and after all that rain there'll be swarm of insects among the trees.'

'The trouble is, young Eve, when you get near water

102

you're inclined to lose your head, not to mention your pants. Can I trust you to be good? Sometimes these rivers run an undertow and I don't want to see you drowned now I've got you this far in one piece.'

'I'll be as good as gold,' she promised eagerly. 'I can read that book you put in your knapsack, and you can get on with your—work.'

'Don't we sound domesticated?' he jeered. 'Right, if you're going to behave yourself, then you can sit by the river and read. Are you wearing a watch?'

'Yes, but it's stopped. I forgot to take it off when I took a bath in the creek.'

'That's what you get for being too eager.' He marched ahead of her into the hut and proceeded to tear a chunk of the mosquito netting so he could wrap the turkey until he had time to pluck it. They placed the vegetables in the iron pot, and Eve asked him if she might borrow his book.

'You're welcome,' he said. 'It's a Carter Dickson, but don't you dare tell me the ending.'

'He's good, isn't he? Thanks.' She caught the book as Wade tossed it. Then he came over and thrust something else into her hand—a packet of nuts and raisins.

'They'll keep up your vitality.' He stood looking down at her, and then, casually, he pushed a stray lock of hair back from her eyes. 'You do realise, Eve, that we're in the middle of a revolt and there may come a moment when I shall have to do to a man what I did to that bird? Out here you do it silently if you can, because a shot can be heard a long way off, and you get the stray rebel who breaks away from the rest, pillaging on his own, or attempting to get back to his family. One of those could come along, so I'm warning you to be

103

on the alert. I'd really prefer to have you where I can keep my eye on you——'

'I'll be all right,' she said quickly. 'I'm not going to think about the black side of things. because that only turns my stomach over and makes me feel nervous.'

'Right. I want to spend at least a couple of hours in the bush and get in as much work as possible, for I shall have to make a rope to tow the tree to the river bank. I shall need the *panga*, so I'm going to trust you with the Breda. Here, take hold of it, it shouldn't be too heavy.'

Eve hesitated, then took the shotgun and found it warm from Wade's skin. 'Am I supposed to use it?' she asked.

'It will give you a feeling of security. If you see anything move, then you get to me as fast as you can. You'll know where I am, for you'll hear me slashing about with the *panga*, cutting off branches from the tree and chopping down vines to make a rope. Keep alert, Eve. Don't get too carried away by the thriller.'

She smiled, and again was struck by the feeling of being so far from all the civilised aspects of her life that they seemed impossibly unreal—lunch with a girl-friend in a Sloane Square bistro, a wander around an art gallery, and maybe a spin into the country for tea-time tennis. None of it bore any relation to what was happening here, two people struggling for existence in a jungle full of dangers that could strike at them without warning.

The river wasn't wide, but it was running at a good pace, and Eve settled down on the plaid robe for a rug, beneath the shade of some canopy banyans. 'A little taste of *laleia*, eh?' Wade said, looking about him with keen eyes, though she felt that it wasn't the flamboyant butterflies he was watching.

'*Laleia?*'

'Paradise—Eden.' He spoke quizzically, but when he looked down at her there was something in his eyes she couldn't quite fathom. 'But don't let it fool you, remember the story of that other Eve and what she found lurking behind a tree.'

He shot a glance at his watch. 'You can stay here an hour, and then the sun will be high, right above you, and you'll come to me, do you hear?'

'Yes, *bwana*,' she said meekly.

'And keep your ears peeled.'

'I will.'

'Um, now I've got to get to work.' He weighed the *panga* in his hand. 'What a stroke of luck they taught me carpentry at that orphanage—carpentry and killing, the requisites of the old pioneers. That's what I feel like, right now—a pioneer about to tackle a bit of husbandry.'

Eve smiled, but her pulses had given an alarming jump, and as if he realised that he had said something a little too meaningful, he turned curtly away from her. 'Be careful, be good,' he said, and a few seconds later he had gone among the sombre towering trees and the green curtains of foliage that fell into place behind his tall figure, the big leaves folding together to intensify Eve's sudden sense of isolation. She chewed a nut and gazed thoughtfully across the river, listening to the sound of birds ... feeling her drumming heart as it slowly quietened down.

It could have been *laleia*, she thought, had there been no rebellion to fear, no other woman to remember, she and Wade alone, letting nothing matter except that he had become her world, the vital heart of it, where nothing would exist but the excitement, the heaven and hunger of being in his arms.

It was a tumultuous truth she could only face for a moment, and then she pushed it resolutely out of mind and bent over the paperback, glad to find that the story was set in London of the pre-war days, when parts of Holborn had been very mysterious. In a while Eve became absorbed in the story, carried away by the mastery of the storyteller ... it was a sudden sense of quiet rather than a sound that touched a warning finger to the base of her spine, sending a sudden shiver through her.

She glanced up slowly, her fingers clenching on the book. The tiny hairs on the nape of her neck were prickling and she sensed instantly that something was standing behind her, ominously still for the moment, but poised to come at her. Her nostrils quivered, but there was no catlike aroma to warn her that a leopard was close to her, so that any sudden movement would be fatal. And she had to turn and look ... she couldn't just sit here and be pounced upon.

As Eve turned to look, she clutched for the Breda and felt the sudden moistness of her hands.

Dark eyes were fixed upon her, raking over her with an intent she understood with sickening clarity ... then he began to move towards her, and Eve knew she must use the Breda and blast him before he got to her. She raised it and it suddenly felt as heavy as lead ... he stood still a moment, the thick lips leering back from the white teeth. It was like one of those awful slow-motion dreams, and then she had her finger on the bolt and was forcing herself to pull it back and release the lead into his face, for it was his face that was so frightening.

The gun fired and the butt kicked hard against her shoulder, but the bullet had flown wild and before she could fire again he was upon her and was wrenching the Breda away from her. Eve felt a terror beyond anything she had ever known ... as a scream ripped from her, he had hold of her and she smelled his sour body odour and saw him swinging the butt of the gun at her head, and even as she ducked he gave a strange liquid cry, his eyes seemed to bulge from their sockets, and then he fell as if pole-axed and Eve saw the knife with its steel blade buried deep in his back, high up where his spine was joined to his neck.

'You okay, lady?' Wade was bending over her, helping her to her feet. She swayed from reaction and was caught to Wade's body, gripped so painfully hard that she almost lost her breath. They stayed like that for several long moments, while the flurried movements of the birds and monkeys settled down until the most persistent sound was that of the flies drawn to that silent form that lay face down on the riverbank, the back of the combat jacket darkly stained where the knife jutted.

'I—I'm a rotten shot,' Eve said shakily. 'But thank God you heard the gun going off.'

'I suppose you got lost in that darn thriller.' He pressed her to him, as if to instil some of his warmth and strength into her. 'Now forget about it, honey, it's over and done with——'

'He came up on me like an animal,' she said, shuddering 'He was upon me almost before I could grab the gun, then my shot went wild a—and all I could see was that awful, savage face—another second and he'd have split my head open.'

Then, driven beyond a force she couldn't control, Eve suddenly flung her arms about Wade's neck and reached for his face with her lips. She felt the tough skin and bone of him, and then he was gripping her hands and forcing her away from him. 'There's no need for that,' he said, roughly. 'I've got to shift this hog out of the way before every fly in the jungle comes buzzing around.'

'You saved my life,' she said simply.

'It's what I'm paid to do,' he rejoined, then bending over the dead body of the insurgent he began to go through his pockets. Eve gnawed her knuckles and gazed down at Wade's dark head ... there was no way to stop what she was feeling for him, for it was right inside her. She watched as he drew out something from one of the pockets of the stained combat jacket and carefully examined it, then with a smile that slashed lines in his brown face he glanced up at Eve.

'This maverick's been following the river route to the coast—see, his map! It bears out my feeling that we couldn't go far wrong if we continued by canoe, but are you still prepared for that? I need time to build the boat, but now we have this map we could trek it, if that's what you want?'

'It's for you to decide, Wade.' She wanted to get away from this place right now, and would have been happy had he decided to pack up then and there. 'Are you going to be able to build the canoe?'

'Sure, that's no problem, but I need a few days to do it in, and this nasty customer might have put you off the idea of staying here while I work on the boat.'

'I'm not that feeble,' she protested, and pushed down inside her the urge to get away without any delay. 'And you know what's best.'

'It would be best for you, Eve, to travel by canoe. And there's food around here, and several wild fruit trees. We can stock up on supplies, and if it's any consolation I'll let you go bathing later on, when the sun cools down a bit.'

'Thanks,' she said drily, and watched as he dragged the rebel into the bush, followed by that gauze of flies. He was gone about ten minutes, and when he returned the knife was back in his belt, and his black hair was damply tousled on his forehead. 'I've stripped the body and buried the clothes,' he said. 'Later on the leopards will make short work of that carcase, and what's left the smaller animals will devour. Now let's see about our own lunch—d'you fancy some baked fish and yams roasted in the fire until their skins crackle?'

Eve stared at him, still deeply shaken herself, but aware that for him the business of killing the enemy was an everyday matter, and her gaze followed him to the river, where he haunched down and cleaned his hands in the water, resting there a moment while the sun dried them.

'We'll head back to camp and get the fish basket and I'll bait it with that piece of pork fat out of the beans. We might be lucky enough to entice a catfish into the trap.'

'Catfish?' she echoed, pulling a face.

'What were you expecting, blue mountain trout?' He swung the Breda on to his shoulder and they entered the dim tunnel of trees that led in the direction of the hut. 'A catfish steak can be very tasty, and you'll be asking the head waiter at the Ritz to put it on the menu when you get back to London.'

'London seems a million miles away,' she murmured. 'Only this seems real, and I can't seem to imagine any more what it's like to sit in a restaurant aimlessly eating a lot of high-priced food and talking a lot of flippant nonsense about life. I don't think I shall ever be the sort of person that I was—I don't want to be, not after this experience.'

'You say that now, Eve, but when you get back to civilisation you'll soon forget your jungle ordeal with a roughneck soldier of fortune.'

'I don't want to forget a single detail,' she protested. 'Nor do I think of you as a roughneck.'

'Come again, lady.' The jeering note came back into his voice. 'Don't go pinning a medal of good conduct on me because I saved your sweet neck. It's all in the line of duty.'

'You can be cynical about it, Wade, but you can't stop me from being grateful to you. You'll never know how frightened I was!'

'Of course I know how you felt, having that brute creep up on you, but don't let the gratitude get all sugared up with hearts and flowers. We're alone together in a ticey situation and I can do without a girl your age getting the idea that it might be romantic to live dangerously with a man in the thousand-tree house.'

'The thousand-tree house?' she echoed.

'The jungle, roofed over as it is by the tall trees laced together at their crowns to form almost a solid green ceiling. We aren't Tarzan and Jane, and don't you forget it. I've made no plans to live in the wilds with a high-society girl.'

'What are your future plans, Wade?' Eve was determined not to let him ruffle her feathers. She was alive because of him, and the very way he talked was an indication that he had a code of honour that made him even more of a hero in her eyes. It made her heart beat fast, admitting to herself that he had come to mean so much to her ... a man whose way of life and commitments to his family meant that he could never be more than her jungle protector. There was nothing beyond Tanga but a parting of their ways.

'I never make plans,' he told her. 'A soldier doesn't go in for that kind of dicing with the gods. He just hopes there isn't a bullet with his name on it.'

Eve felt a clutch of dismay deep inside her and wished she had the right to hold him fast and be the woman who could stop him from being a soldier.

'Oh, but you must have a dream in your heart,' she said. 'Everyone has a longing for something that will give them peace or pleasure or a sense of security.' I bet you'd love a farm! A place in the country, with a couple of horses in the stable, some pigs and cows, and a few crop acres. Go on, Wade, tell me I'm wrong.'

'Dreams are for the young,' he rejoined, 'and I mean to see that my son gets his dream. He exists because of me. He deserves to have a good life, and it's what I've fought for—killed for.'

Wade looked down suddenly at Eve and his eyes were steely and uncompromising as the knife in his belt. 'I've waded in slaughter—you just keep remembering that and you'll soon forget any foolish notion that I could reap and sow and be a farmer.'

'I bet you'd love it,' she argued.

'Love?' His face was hard as nails. 'What would a young thing like you know about love? What would a

111

mercenary have in common with all the tender delights of loving anything?'

'There's your son—your wife,' Eve said quietly. 'Wouldn't they like to have you home all the time?'

'What is this?' he demanded. 'It's like some damn interview for *True Confessions*!'

He marched ahead of her into the rondavel and found the fish basket and the piece of pork fat he had saved for bait. 'You can stay here and do some tidying up,' he said. 'I shan't be too long, and this time keep your wits about you and keep the Breda close to hand. I don't think another insurgent can be hanging about or that gunshot would have flushed him out. I'll chop you off some of those big rubbery leaves and you can do a spot of sweeping out with them.'

'All right,' she said, and couldn't stop herself from casting a nervous look around the compound.

'To hell with it.' His hand closed on her shoulder, his fingers pressing into her slight bones. 'You can come with me to the river if you promise not to pester me with questions. My private life is none of your business, young lady, and if you'll bear that in mind, we'll get along.'

'I'll stay here,' she shook free of his hand. 'The hut does need a sweep out if we're going to be using it for the next few days.'

'Are you sure, now?' He handed her the Breda. 'If it gives you the willies to be here alone, then you say so.'

'It's something I've got to get used to.' Eve tilted her chin and gripped the gun. 'I can't be at your elbow all the time you're working on the boat—men don't like that, do they? They like to get on with the job.'

'What would you know about men, apart from that

112

honourable stick you're pledged to marry?' He suddenly smiled, a quirk of the lip and eyebrow. 'Keep your pecker up and next time shoot straight at the body and don't hesitate for a second. In this game, honey, it's them or us. 'Bye for now.'

He marched off leaving her alone, but for several minutes she was unable to relax and just stood there, letting her eyes search every ruined mound where a hut had stood, every tree that cast a shadow in the sun. She listened to the monkeys chattering away, and to the birds calling and flying in the treetops. While there were animal sounds she could be fairly certain that nothing on two legs was creeping through the bush, but all the same it would be a long time before she banished from her mind that incident by the river.

She set to work on the hut, clearing out everything so she could give the floor and walls a thorough brushdown with the big leaves Wade had cut for her. They had thick stems and made quite serviceable brooms, and by the time she was finished quite a bit of the dirt had been swept outside and she had slaughtered several large insects.

During the course of her housework she would pause every so often and listen for those reassuring squeals and thrashings among the trees, and in a while she was actually laughing as one of the monkeys began to hurl big squashy bananas at her, red-skinned things that she didn't much like the look of. However, she decided to try one and found it eatable, if a trifle on the syrupy side.

The sun was really high now and she wiped a sleeve across her moist face. She longed for that bathe Wade had promised her, but she knew she must abide by his decision that it would be best when the sun began to decline and the benefits of a bathe would be all the sweeter. To take a plunge while the sun was high would only mean that within a short while they'd both be sweating again.

He was an exasperating man, but he knew his way about in this tough, menacing world, and Eve smiled to herself as she sat on her bundle and chewed sweet banana. Sunshine splashed across the compound like hot rain, and she would have loved a drink of water, but knew it had to be boiled first and their fire was dead.

What would have been her reaction to him had they met in normal circumstances? At a party, say, where he strolled in looking dark and distinctive in a dinner-suit, immaculate poplin shirt and cummerbund, casting casual grey eyes around the room and letting them fasten upon her in a dress all frilled and floaty. Would he have noticed her? Would he have liked the Eve of those days, bandbox-fresh and not unattractive with her gay young mouth, and her skin looking creamy against the Titian glint of her hair?

But even had they met like that, there was still his wife in the background ... the woman he was bound to, whom he seemed to avoid talking about. Had their marriage gone all wrong from the start, as forced marriages so often did? Was he resentful that she had caught him with the oldest trick in the book, inducing him to lose his head over her, letting herself fall for his child so he'd feel obliged to marry her?

Eve decided that Wade would resent being forced into a corner, but all the same he had stood by the woman he had married, and he obviously cared a great deal for his son. Did he carry a picture of Larry? Eve longed to know. She longed to find out for herself if Wade's son resembled him.

She found herself staring at his knapsack, which she had propped against a tree. Had she time to take a look in his crocodile-skin wallet which he kept attached to his pouch of medications and other handy items by means of an elastic band? It seemed a sly thing to do, yet she was driven by a need not only to see a photograph of his son, but possibly one of his wife as well. With a quick-beating pulse she bent over the battered knapsack and undid the straps. Her hand went inside and rapidly located the oilskin pouch and wallet; she detached the wallet and opened the flap, searching inside with fingers that trembled. Her fingertips felt the edge of a snapshot and she drew it out ... oh yes, this was Larry, and he was good-looking, with a shock of untidy black hair, keen, well-set eyes gazing directly ahead, and the lean, rather serious face of the student.

Wade's son ... but much as she searched Eve couldn't find a snapshot of Wade's wife.

'What an inquisitive young lady you are, foraging about in a man's belongings when his back is turned! I'm sure you were brought up to be better-mannered than that.'

Eve crouched by the knapsack and felt the hot embarrassment sweep over her. She was caught out and no mistake, and as she felt Wade take a stride and halt beside her, her nerves fluttered madly. 'Did you find what you were looking for?' he drawled. He leaned down and plucked the photograph of Larry from her nerveless fingers. 'Curious to find out if he was as good-looking as I said?'

'He's a fine young man,' Eve said huskily. 'You must be very proud of him.'

'He's the best part of me—what else were you searching for, lady? A portrait of my wife?'

Eve quivered as if the tip of a lash had flicked her skin, and involuntarily she glanced up at Wade. His teeth were bared for a moment in a half-savage smile, and as her face grew hot and pink the devil was agitated in his eyes.

'May I have my wallet?' he requested.

Silently she handed it to him and he replaced the snapshot of his son. 'I'd have shown it to you had you asked,' he said. 'Fathers get a kick out of showing off their offspring to people.'

'I—it was wrong of me to pry into your wallet,' Eve said humbly. 'I don't know what came over me.'

'I think I know.' He tucked the wallet away, and the next instant had hold of Eve by the wrist. 'It had something to do with this.' As he spoke he dragged her against him and she could feel his other hand gripping her so that her shirt was drawn up to expose her tingling spine. He plucked her close to him and took her shaking lips in a long punishing kiss ... a kiss like no other she had ever experienced, so unrelenting that she felt her lips going molten under his mouth ... felt a tumult of her senses that quickened into an excitement that made her clutch at him.

Hard and hungry grew the lips that searched her face, her neck, the strong hand cupping her head while he moved his mouth over her flushed skin, his other hand roaming her shoulders and moving down her back to where her body was bare.

He clasped her slenderness to every hard line of him

and seemed careless of all danger now he had her in his arms. Eve was shaken to the core by what she felt, and what she had aroused in him. He suddenly lifted her and seemed to be seeking a place to lay her down— coming to his senses the very next instant, his breath raking hot across her face.

'Get away from me!' He thrust her away from him, not roughly or cruelly, but firmly.

'Oh, Wade——' She just managed his name, and found herself leaning against a tree, while he stood dragging a hand across his face.

The static was still alive in her veins. She had felt a deep falling-through-time into a lush, heady sweetness she had wanted with all her body, every inch of her skin, every throb of her heart. Her lips were still burning as she drew her tongue around them.

'You live up to your name, don't you?' he growled. 'You had to let yourself be tempted, and couldn't wait to let loose the devil in me. D'you think I'll let it happen a second time? Not on your sweet life I won't! If I get you to Tanga, I'll get you there intact and still innocent enough to fool your bridegroom.'

'Y—you kissed me——' she said weakly.

'You were asking for it, and I'm not made of iron-wood. Well, now you know what could happen to you, so from now on lay off being curious about my love life.'

Eve lowered her eyes from his face and couldn't stop her gaze from dwelling on his hands clenched at his thighs. She had been held to the tempered steel of that lithe, jungle-toughened body ... her heart was longing for more of him and he was thrusting her away and telling her to keep her distance.

The ebbs and flows of passion had swept over her and she felt strangely weak and unlike herself. Her pulses leapt so unsteadily and her heart pounded so furiously, not even when the rebel had crept up on her had she felt this degree of agitation ... this loss of self-possession, so that she hardly knew what to do with herself.

'What would it matter to anyone,' she heard herself say, 'if we made love?'

'It would matter, little one, if in your ineffable innocence you fell for a baby. Grow up, Eve!' His voice hardened. 'If I made love to you, I'd go every inch of the way—I couldn't stop myself, with you!'

His eyes swept her up and down. 'You're made for a youngster, all shining ideals and no dark shadows in his life. A boy you can have fun with, and grow up with eye to eye, without having to wonder about his past. Don't ask me to rob that boy by taking the frosting off his angel cake—I could do it, Eve, and then you'd learn all about the hell of regret.'

'I'd regret nothing—with you,' she said, her arms flung out at either side of her, her hands gripping the tree, something defenceless and yet enticing in the attitude she had taken, the neck of her green shirt pulled to one side to reveal the whiteness of her skin.

'You don't know what you're saying—you're talking like a foolish, romantic kid on her first date,' he said, taking a deep hard breath and thrusting the black hair from his moist brow. 'I saved your neck, so you feel you owe me something—you don't owe me a thing, Eve, least of all that sweet, innocent body of yours. Stop flaunting it! We've got other fish to fry—or should I say bake?'

He turned away from her and began taking fish from the basket, which he had already cleaned and gutted down by the river. 'Will you collect some dry wood so we can start the fire?' he said casually.

But she couldn't move, all she could do was say dreamily: 'I don't care about anyone but you.'

'What about my wife?' Wade asked, and it was as if he drove a knife into Eve. 'What of my son? Don't they count when the pretty deb wants a new kind of toy to amuse herself with?'

'Oh, don't be cruel to me!' She flung out a hand in a gesture of defence against the way he wounded her.

'I'm being realistic. You're just giving way to a romantic urge. It's nothing more than that, but it's dangerous. Were you an experienced woman of the world, I'd probably take you and not care a tinker's curse, but you're half my age and you're in my charge. Sister Mercy knows it. That good nun left you in my keeping and I won't commit a blasphemy by breaking faith with her. Now collect that wood and stop moon- ing about. I'm darned hungry!'

Aching, desolate, Eve moved about on the edge of the compound collecting small branches of wood. It couldn't be true, could it, that she was never going to know again the passionate delight of finding herself in Wade's fierce embrace?

She wanted it, that sweet shuddering she couldn't control ... that swooning into such an acute aliveness. She wanted to give herself to him, for there was no shining youth awaiting her in England, only marriage to James because her guardian wanted it. Why couldn't she have Wade for this little time that was left, and know at least what it felt like to belong to a real man?

119

But she had come up against something inexorable in that hard, warrior's nature of his ... his strange reverence for that big silver cross worn by Sister Mercy.

He'd crucify the pair of them rather than destroy the good nun's faith in him.

He had admitted that he was a Catholic, part of a faith that didn't recognise divorce. Eve was certain he didn't love his wife, but that wouldn't stop him from remaining her husband, no matter what he might feel for someone else.

Eve thought of the way he had kissed *her*. Passionately ... madly. But such passion didn't have to be meaningful for a man who probably hadn't been alone with an Englishwoman for some time. She had to face that and couldn't let herself be carried away by a few mad kisses into the realms of fantasy. Wade was very much a man and the touch of a woman would fire him ... that was all it had been. That was the bleak truth of the matter and she had to accept it.

'Will this be enough?' She dumped the wood on the ground beside him.

'Fine, thanks.' He shot a glance at her, then slowly lowered his left eyelid in a wink. 'Here's looking at you, kid,' he murmured.

Eve turned away from him, her own eyes flooding with the silly emotional tears. Why did he have to be bound to some other woman, this tough and tantalising man who made James seem like a languid, bloodless shadow?

Eve gave a sorrowful, angry shake of her head so that the tears flew off her cheeks. She was a woman and she knew she could make him lose his head if she tried, but that wouldn't solve anything ... it might make him despise her, and she would sooner be his jungle pal and have him wink at her in that matey way than have him regard her as no better than those loose women in garrison towns to whom soldiers turned for brief consolation.

Brushing quickly at her cheek, Eve turned back to him. 'Can I do anything to help?' she asked.

'Sure, you can go and get the yams. In just a little while, lady, you're going to have a tasty meal inside you. How's that strike you?'

'It couldn't be better at the Ritz,' she replied, watching a moment as he laid the fish on the fire stones. 'All we need is the wine list.'

'You're forgetting the coconut,' he said. 'We'll open that and make believe it's a vintage wine—a fine white one.'

She smiled and knew the game had to be played this way ... the other way was too dangerous, even though it could have been rather heavenly.

CHAPTER SEVEN

ON the river earlier it had been cool, but now the sun was like a molten flame above them, and the sweat had plastered Wade's shirt to his body, clinging darkly to his chest and shoulders as he thrust the paddle in and out of the water that glistened like thick oil in the sunlight.

Wade had worked with vandalistic zeal on the boat, spending tireless hours shaping and carving the storm-felled tree which he had dragged to the riverbank by means of a long rope woven from plaited vines.

With each passing day Eve's admiration for his industry, guts and skill had increased until she began to feel an almost frightening idolatry for the man. She had never known anyone like him in her life … a life which until now had been filled with ease and comfort provided by well-paid servants. She had never seen her guardian lift a log on to the fire, let alone create a boat from the trunk of a tree.

She had watched Wade at work with a feeling of akin to awe, and on the morning they loaded the canoe and the craft glided out on to the surface of the river, the certainty was strong in her that she could never be persuaded to marry James. She would never marry at all, least of all an effete young stockbroker who could do nothing except sit behind a desk and buy and sell shares for his clients. As his wife she would be no more than an adornment gracing his Maida Vale house, there to entertain the wives of his business associates, and to spend the evenings dining with James' relatives, with the occasional weekend in the country for some golf, riding or shooting, according to the season.

The prospect wasn't to be borne, and if she must inevitably say goodbye to Wade, how could she ever forget being with him in the jungle? Sometimes she reflected back on her very first sight of him, when he had seemed so hard and unmerciful in the way he drove the nuns and herself through the bush to the airfield bungalow. She had thought him without sympathy or feeling, but she had learned since that he was rather like an iceberg, with depths to his character she would have loved to explore.

Oh God, sometimes it seemed as if she were thinking and loving like some heroine in a romantic story. She had never believed in that kind of love, but now discovered that it did exist. But she guarded it and was careful not to let it show in her eyes. For her sake and his she acted the boy, never complaining of the enervating heat, ever ready to do his bidding, keeping as bright and perky as his cabin-boy. It amused him, but sometimes there seemed a shadow of concern in his eyes when they played over her, for she had grown thinner, even more fine-boned on their diet of fish, fruit, and the constant tension of what might be lurking around each bend of the river.

They had no way of knowing if Tanga had fallen to rebel hands, and each mile was bringing them closer to their destination.

Now and again on a smooth stretch he allowed her to paddle for a while, so that she kept supple and didn't grow stiff crouched all the time on the low seat which he had fashioned, with a bar across so that she could hold on when they ran into the rapids caused by the sudden cascades of water raining down like liquid silver from great escarpments of rock. Some of the river scenery was breathlessly beautiful, where the most exotic flowers grew against the curtains of green foliage; and never had Eve imagined such colourful birds, some of them sheer blue, darting on the water and emerging with big fish flapping in their beaks. It seemed incredible at times that they were two people hurrying towards a refuge . . . or a town already occupied by savage, undisciplined rebels.

'What shall we do,' Eve asked Wade, 'if Tanga has fallen to the rebels?'

'Cut and run,' he had replied. 'Get the hell out and head for some place that might still be in Government hands.'

It both frightened and excited her, the thought that she and Wade might be alone like this for an indefinite period. She might act the boy, and it might amuse him to let her, but there were underlying currents to the situation that couldn't be ignored. When they camped in the evenings and bathed in the river, it was impossible to pretend that he didn't see her, nude and pale-honey, pulling herself from the water, her limbs dripping in the light of the moon that had risen a few nights ago, to hang in the sky like a globe of witchfire.

It was equally impossible to pretend that she didn't see him, like some weathered figure of bronze, some pagan deity emerging from the river.

There just wasn't room for the modesties of civilised living. They couldn't exist as they did and be unaware of each other.

Eve knew exactly how the thick dark hair grew in an arrow straight down Wade's lean, strong body, and she had seen that fearful scar on his thigh, almost deep enough to thrust in her hand. She knew that he must be aware of the velvety mole on her left hip, and her much smaller and neater scar from an appendix removal when she was fourteen years old.

Such an awareness of each other could be borne if it were only for a short while longer, but if it continued, in the moist, musky, sensual jungle, then one dusky evening the inevitable would happen, he would reach for her and Eve would be helpless to resist him. She would submit to the excitement and ruthlessness she had already felt in his embrace, and alone with him in the wild, lush heart of Africa she would give way without reserve to being a woman. The very thought was enough to make her tingle from the nape of her neck to the soles of her feet, and she had to look away from Wade, for the movement of his brown arms, the dark wet clinging of his shirt to his muscular skin was enough to melt her on the inside as the hot sun was wilting her on the outside.

She longed for the evening when they tied up the canoe and rested; ate their supper after their bathe, and lounged beside the fire talking quietly of impersonal things. There was a domesticity to it that could have led easily to the intimacy she both wanted and feared. If he touched her, if he took her, driven to it by all that was primitive in their surroundings, Eve knew it would be a heaven followed by hell when he told her, as adamantly as before, that he wasn't free to keep her.

It had to be everything or nothing. Eve realised that each time she looked at Wade. She couldn't surrender herself to him and then give him up with a sweet, sacrificing smile. But she could just endure the parting that must come if she never knew what it was like to be his possession ... she had come the hard way to that realisation, much as she longed for the feel of his mouth on hers again, the caress of his hands, the loving of his lean body, certain and tireless at his handling of the canoe.

Eve shivered in the heat, torn between the longing and the martyrdom of loving a man who belonged to another woman.

'Your hands keeping all right?' he asked suddenly, for during that early spell of coolness he had allowed her to paddle for a while.

Eve glanced at them and gave a grin. They were brown, nail-torn, and were developing slight callouses across the palms. 'They got hardened at the mission,' she said. 'I told you I did the scrubbing, and also I peeled buckets of vegetables for the patients. I wonder is Sister Mercy and the others are back in England, or still working out here?'

'My bet is that they're still out here,' he replied. 'While someone needs them, those saintly creatures will carry on regardless.'

Eve's smile deepened, for in that moment she had caught the Irish inflection in Wade's voice, which he must have picked up years ago from his father. Then she turned her head and her smile faded and unaware she trailed her hand in the water ... were he not a Catholic, would he cut free from his wife?

'Take your hand out of the water,' he snapped. 'There's no knowing what's under the surface, and if you lost some fingers I'd have one hell of a job keeping you free of infection.'

'Sorry.' She guiltily pulled her fingers free of the water. 'I wasn't thinking.'

'No, you were miles away in thoughts of England, no doubt, and your fine wedding day at some smart church with lots of guests and bags of rice.'

Eve didn't protest that he had it all wrong, and that she'd fight her guardian yet again if he tried to force her into a loveless marriage. Perhaps she'd go into a nunnery herself, train for the life and then return to Africa to work under Sister Mercy for the rest of her days. Why not? It seemed a more worthwhile prospect than settling into a useless rut with a man she didn't care for.

Dusk always came suddenly, after the clashing of colours around the dying sun, and then the clamorous sound of water fowl would follow. Wade pulled into a clearing, and Wade stood a moment against the afterglow in the sky, tall, unbowed despite his long day at the paddle, pulling his sleeve across his forehead. 'If I had to do this all over again,' he remarked, 'surprisingly enough I'd choose to do it with you, Eve. What a trip to remember, eh? If you ever take a world cruise on a luxury liner, think back on these days and nights and you might laugh or weep.'

'I shan't laugh,' she replied, watching him, letting her gaze travel up the long legs in combat khaki to the hard, inflexible shoulders and the life-hardened face. 'I was thinking earlier on that I might decide to train for mission work——'

'What?' he broke in. 'What the devil do you mean—be a nun?'

'Why not?' she asked. 'Others do it, so why not me?'

'You haven't the right temperament.' He said it almost scornfully.

127

'Thanks, Major. You're always ready to boost my ego.'

'To the devil with it, Eve, you aren't a cold, devout saint, and you know it. Forget such nonsense and do what you were born to do.'

'And what's that?' she enquired. 'Develop from the season's debutante into the cool and gracious hostess of a house kept spotless by maids, and a kitchen ruled over by some treasure of a cook who won't even allow me to boil an egg.'

'That doesn't have to happen,' he said, almost curtly. 'You have gumption enough not to be forced into marriage if you don't love the man. Find someone you can love, even if he happens to be poor. That way you'll soon learn how to boil an egg.'

'Thanks,' she said again. 'I suppose this little lecture means that we're only a few miles from Tanga?'

'You've guessed it, Eve. This time tomorrow you might be on a plane and on your way home—all being well and if we find the *status quo* at Tanga.'

'What happens if we don't?' Eve could feel the agitation of her pulses, and the sudden twisting pain deep inside her, as if already the strands that had bound her to Wade for this strange journey were now beginning to tear asunder.

'Then we're still up the river, but fortunately with a paddle.' He leapt ashore and quickly secured the canoe to the thick roots of a tree. Eve followed him and thought dismally that this might be their last night together, their last bathe in the river, their final supper all smoky from the campfire they dared to light even though it might be a beacon for the enemy. He was fatalistic in some ways, was Wade O'Mara, but he was also too much a soldier to be capable of the kind of fear other men might have felt. He had weaned the fear out of Eve, and she was ever certain that if a band of insurgents fell upon them and the odds were too great, Wade would turn the Breda upon her and she would die at his hands. It was the way she wanted to die, if she had to.

He got the fire going, and Eve baked some fish, squeezed wild lemon over it and sliced a wild cucumber. For dessert they had big squashy berries with coconut jelly, which was rather delicious from the green nuts which Wade climbed for, cutting them down with his *panga*. Watching him do certain things Eve wondered at the difference between him and men like her guardian, not all that much older than Wade and yet grown flabby and reliant on other people for every sort of need. Such men would starve in the jungle, go out of their heads, and not be able to tell a suspended hornet's nest from a shaggy fruit. Of course, seated in importance behind their city desks, they were big men, and would regard someone like Wade as a barbarian.

Her dear barbarian, she thought, worth a thousand of the kind of people she must go back to. Oh lord, how to explain all this to the man who had reared her, paid her school fees, sent her abroad to acquire the poise of a young woman expected to marry well? How to convince him that she could never marry anyone chosen by him? They'd fight again, and she had the feeling she might burst into tears the next time; weep wildly for the man she had left behind in Africa.

Somewhere close by the clearing where they camped a parrot bird was still awake and apparently watching them in the glow of the fire. All at once it moved along its branch and sqawked what sounded like: 'Your dinner . . . your dinner!'

They laughed in unison. 'Some dinner,' Eve murmured. 'A pity all the yams are used up, they were delicious all hot and crackling on the outside and so white and flavoursome inside.'

'You'll be dining at some swanky restaurant in no time at all, gobbling *coq au vin* and pears in brandy.' Wade lay full stretch on the blanket and smoked one of his hand-rolled cigarettes. Overhead spread the branches of a great forest tree, and above them was the sky washed with moonlight, with clusters of stars in the shadowy patches.

'Why do you take it for granted that I shall slot back so easily into my old life?' she asked, seated there in the firelight with her arms about her updrawn knees. They had been lazy tonight and had not yet bathed in the river, as if they were waiting for the moon to ride right over them, casting the river to silver before they plunged in.

'You'll do so, little lady, because you aren't old.' His dark brows had a devilish twist to them. 'Want your sweetie?'

'I wish it was! I could just go for a nice sticky caramel, but instead I have to chew on that awful-tasting tablet that's supposed to keep me from getting dried up and saltless.'

'You'll never be saltless.' He handed her the tablet. 'And I never could tolerate sugary females.'

'Do I accept that as a compliment?' she asked, chewing the tablet and washing it down with hot smoky coffee, made from wild beans which Wade had roasted and ground to powder between a couple of stones. 'And have you taken your own tablet?'

'I'm salty enough,' he drawled, blowing a smoke ring. 'I want you fighting fit when I get you to Tanga, the saints willing. Got your story all prepared for your stern guardian?'

'Did I say he was stern?' Eve forced a smile to her lips, but again she felt that dropping sensation in her stomach, as if very gradually all the elation was going out of her life.

'I have the feeling he expects you to conform, eh? I imagine he's chosen your prospective bridegroom, but don't be bulldozed into the fellow's arms, not if you don't want to run into them.'

'James is all right,' she said, making her voice casual. 'I could do worse, I suppose, but he's the kind who would expect me to drape myself in pretty clothes and chatter with equally useless friends and sit on a committee or two, so long as I didn't overtax my bird brains. The upper classes remain very conservative in their ideas—they aren't like you, Wade. They don't go out and *do*. They couldn't do half the things you're capable of—if I were lost in the jungle with James, I'd be in a pretty poor way by now.'

'Are you saying I've spoiled you for other men?' Wade asked sardonically. 'In the literal sense, you understand. No one can say I've had more than a nibble of the sweet white frosting.'

'Are you cynical about everything?' Eve murmured, her fingers clenching together until they hurt. 'Despite the dangers, this has been one of the best experiences of my life. I shall never forget it.'

'Nor I, lady.' He rolled to one side so he was facing her and their eyes met and held, then broke apart. 'There's been a certain alchemy, but don't mistake it for anything else. When you're home again, and you take up the threads of the life meant for you, you'll gradually forget all this and in a few months' time you won't even remember my face. I guarantee it, Eve.'

'And you'll take up the threads of your life, I suppose?'

'Sure, I shall go on fighting out here until things are in order again, then I shall probably take a holiday with my—family, and then I'll find another war to fight.'

'Don't you ever want to settle down?' Eve kept her gaze on the fire because she felt that her eyes were bleak. A holiday with his family, he had said. It made her feel so cut off from him; it underlined what she was, just a girl he had brought through the jungle to the threshold of safety, doing his very best for her, aware that she thought him valorous and daring, and letting her down as lightly as possible. Soldiers must often come up against this kind of hero-worship, Eve supposed. It wouldn't be the first time in his life, but it was the first time in hers, and she saw an awful, lonely future ahead of her . . . if she couldn't forget him.

'I've been too many years a fighting man,' he said, tossing the stub of his cigarette into the fire. 'Maybe when I'm really decrepit, they'll offer me a cot at the Chelsea Hospital.'

'Oh, Wade!' It was a cry from the heart she couldn't suppress. 'You make me want to cry when you talk like that. As if your family——'

'It's all right,' he soothed, 'I'm only jesting. Shall we go and cool off in the river, lady? That moon up there is big as an uncut cheese and I fancy a moon-swim—a sort of pagan farewell to all this. Are you game?'

Eve didn't have to be asked twice, and collecting their towels and the soap they shared, and not forgetting the Breda, they hastened to the water that was rippling silver in the radiance of the moon. A big gauzy moth brushed Eve's cheek and she could feel a primitive response to the night in the very centre of her being. The white fire up there must have confused the cicadas, for they were vibrating madly in the trees, and she breathed the musky scent of a night-flowering plant.

'Get thee behind a tree, temptress,' Wade grinned, and planted her behind a huge silk-cotton where she swiftly removed every stitch, but was careful to hang slacks, shirt and briefs on a branch before running eagerly into the water.

Wade was already swimming about, and Eve felt the combined thrill of the cool water and sharing it with him. She rubbed the soap over herself and rinsed off the suds, then swam over to Wade and handed him the depleted bar.

'What a night, eh?' His teeth gleamed in a smile. 'We couldn't have asked for more on our last night together, except for music drifting across the river.'

'What a romantic idea!' Eve moved her arms in a lazy backstroke, uncaring that the silvery light glimmered on her pale body. Wade was a husband and father; he didn't have to pretend that he didn't know what a woman looked like. Nor did she pretend to herself that she wasn't playing the temptress. This was the last time they'd swim together (if all was well at Tanga) and she knew what she wanted to happen ... she wanted a lasting memory to take back to England.

Her fingertips touched Wade and she felt the shock of it vibrate through him ... then he somersaulted with hardly a splash, a gleaming body that was moonlit, with a dark clouding of hair that brushed Eve as he swam up beneath her and wrapped his arms all the way around her. It was incredibly sensuous, wonderful, the feel of his hands gliding over her wet curves.

'Eve, you little devil,' he groaned. 'God, how lovely you feel, like a slim white fish with soft, velvety scales all alight and trembling. I'm mad for you, you wicked child. I want you till you cry the jungle down—but I'm damn well not going to do what Adam did!'

'Scared?' she taunted, slipping her arms around him and feeling his body taut and burning through the cool water. 'Is the great big hero a mouse at heart? Oh, love me, love me, Wade, so I'll have something I can't forget!'

'You'd have it all right.' He scooped her into his arms and ploughed out of the water with her and dropped her to her feet on the riverbank. His hand slapped out and stung her wet bottom. 'Now stop being a pretty strumpet and behave yourself. I've been a gentleman with you for the first time in my inglorious life and I'm not spoiling the sheet.'

'Is this what they give medals for?' she jeered. 'I've seen it on its grimy ribbon. What did they give it for? Gallant action in the mess?'

'Stop it!' He gripped her slippery shoulders and gave her a hard shake. 'It would be the easiest thing in the world to throw you down on my army blanket and love the breath out of you, all the way, Eve, to that moon up there, and then down in the mud. You'd find yourself with a baby in that slim white body, and I'd be the father, and unable to marry you! Have sense. Be realistic. Get dressed!'

'I want a baby.' She clung to him like catchweed in the streaming moonlight, her wet skin clinging to his.

'I want yours—a black-haired boy like the one you gave that other woman. Why not? I'm entitled to something of yours, if she's going to have you till you—till you get what you seem to be after, a bullet in your heart.'

Her hand played down his chest and her fingers went into that awful cicatrice in his flesh. 'I've never known a real man in my life—oh, Wade, there'll never be another night like this one, and we'll never be alone like this ever again. Someone will make a woman of me, if I ever marry, and I want you to do it. *I want you.*'

He held her, as if lost for words, and Eve loved the rough and tender heaven of his arms. 'Right,' his voice was low and savage against her neck. 'I want you—because you're young and pretty and innocent. I want to make a feast of you, here in the jungle. I want to kiss every bit of you and let my body revel in you—but I'd hate my own guts in the morning, and I might even hate you, my vixen, for letting me do all that to you. Go home to England, Eve, sweet and untroubled, so I can remember you like that. How do you think I could live, not knowing if you were having my kid, or laid out in some clinic having it taken away? Do you think your upper-crust guardian would let his ward have the baby of a mercenary? Think again, my pretty Eve. A girl might hide what's in her heart, but there's no hiding a baby.'

'You seem so certain I'd get—that way.'

'There's a good chance of it.' His eyes slid down the smooth length of her bare body, and she felt the tensing of his forearm muscles under her gripping hand. In the light of the moon his face might have been carved, except for the flicker of a muscle near his mouth. 'I've

135

been living hard for some time, honey, and I don't think I'd keep a cool head if I had you at my mercy. Come, you're not so innocent that you don't know what I mean?'

'I—I know what you mean,' she said huskily. 'Doesn't it count, Wade, that I'm ready to take the consequences?'

'Don't talk nonsense.' His voice grated. 'You're little older than my Larry, a mere girl with all your life ahead of you. Think I'd spoil that for you? My life has made me hard and I've done things I shall never talk about, but I haven't come to robbing the cradle, not yet I haven't, and I'd put the Breda to your head if anyone out here tried it on and I didn't have a chance of protecting you any other way. You know that, so go and put some clothes on and let a guy's blood pressure settle down.'

'Oh, Wade——!' Eve raised a hand and pushed the damp rumpled hair back from his brow. 'You are merciless, aren't you? Y—you won't let me thank you for all you've done for me.'

'I'll have thanks enough when I see you safely on that plane to England.' Taking forcible hold of her wrists he held her away from him, and Eve felt the coldness where the warmth had been. Oh God, where else was she going to find a man so exciting, so sure in his strength, so self-reliant? All around them the countless fireflies danced in the air, spots of green fire, and Eve could feel the love inside her, burning away discretion and pride like flame through steel. She trembled and knew that she could dissolve Wade's inflexibility even yet; her wrist tensed in his hand, and her eyes were sheerest gold, sensuous as a cat's as they dwelt on his face.

'Your grip is hurting me,' she said softly.

He let go at once and her hand was free ... time seemed to stand still and she knew he was reading her eyes, waiting for her to make her move. Emotion throbbed between them as the jungle throbbed all around them, the air filled with the moist, overpowering incense of forest foliage and milky vines.

He was watching her, daring her to go ahead with what her topaz eyes threatened. He knew, just as she did, that she could tempt him and make him weak as water, and at the same time awesomely strong. The devil whispered in her ear and wild, sweet heaven was only inches from her grasp.

She turned away from him, shudderingly. She couldn't have her heaven and risk him hating her afterwards ... he had his son to consider, and even if his wife didn't possess his heart, she did have legal rights that he would abide by. That was the kind of man he was. Tenacious and loyal and strong-willed. For these qualities Eve loved him ... it wasn't just physical, what she felt for her mercenary Major.

Eve suffered a moment, silent and intense, then she walked away to where she had left her clothes, and there behind the silk-cotton tree she rubbed her body with the towel and dressed herself. The magic had ebbed away and now she felt rather tired, and aware of meshes of thorny growth around her, and immense night-hung webs knobbed with hairy black spiders. some of them hideously huge and tinged with red on their crooked legs. She shivered and no longer did the jungle seem romantic to her ... her heart was cold and

137

she wanted the final few miles to Tanga to be covered as soon as possible.

She reached for her towel, which she had flung aside on a bush, and as she took hold of it felt a sharp stab of pain as a thorn ripped her thumb, tearing the flesh where it was latched to the nail. The pain was so acute that tears came into her eyes and she felt a salty taste in her mouth.

'You dressed, Eve?' Wade came to her side, dressed himself with his hair slicked back, and forcing herself to ignore the pain of her torn thumbnail, she nodded and walked with him through the moonlight tangled in the trees to where their campfire burned beneath the humming kettle.

'Fancy some more coffee?' he asked. 'Or will it keep you awake?'

'I am rather thirsty,' she replied, and felt certain her thoughts of him were going to keep her from sleeping. It was unbearable that they were soon to part, and abstractedly she placed her thumb between her lips and sucked the sore place where the thorn had jabbed and torn. She tasted blood, but wouldn't examine the small wound in case Wade noticed. He had warned her more than once that the slightest scratch in the jungle could become infectious if it wasn't treated right away. But she couldn't have borne his concern, his doctoring of her thumb ... his hands upon her.

She sat down on her plaid bundle and gazed into the fire. Better that they stay polite with each other, thrusting away all personal contact. She wasn't ashamed that she had wanted him to make love to her; she didn't care that she had thrown aside her pride and revealed how she felt about him, but somehow, from somewhere, she had to find the courage to walk away from him when the time came, and right now her courage was at such low ebb that the smallest show of sympathy would have reduced her to a weeping heap that would have exasperated him. Men so hated tears, and she didn't want Wade's last memory of her to be a maudlin one.

He made the coffee and they shared the mug, and they were sitting there quietly when both of them caught the sound of something rustling in the bush.

Eve tensed and she saw Wade sit up, turn his head and stare intently into those wicked green shadows. Her heartbeats quickened and her nostrils pulled into them the bitter, nutty tang of the wood fire. She saw Wade's hand grip the Breda and she knew that he was alert in every nerve, making hardly any sound as he climbed to his feet. He moved the shotgun into a firing position and with a tread as wary as a cat's he moved towards the bush, and Eve wanted to cry out to him not to go in there where a black tracery of fronds and branches made it so dark and menacing.

But she couldn't cry out, she could only watch in silence and fear for him. He was gone and there was darkness where he had been, and Eve gazed at the emptiness with stricken eyes, every fibre of her body straining forward, ready to leap and join him should it be a human who had made those stealthy sounds of movement.

The moments passed and the silence was filled in by the low harsh purring of the cicadas, and the trilling and croaking of tree-frogs. So intensely concentrated was Eve's attitude that she could feel herself trembling, and she could feel pain jabbing the nerves of her left hand, where the thick sharp thorn had stabbed her.

'It's all right.' Wade came back to her, moving without stealth this time. 'I couldn't smell cat, so I think it must have been a wild pig roaming about, grubbing for roots, I expect.'

Eve couldn't answer him, her teeth were clenched and her body was in the grip of a tension that wouldn't relax. Wade leaned over her and laid his hand on her shoulder, a touch she felt to the bottom of her spine. 'Come on,' he chided her, 'don't get the jitters over a funny old pig——'

'W—what if it had been a human one?' she demanded, and she flung back her head and looked up at him wildly. 'How can you be sure? W—we could be surrounded by them!'

'I'd know, Eve.' He haunched down, cradled his Breda in one arm, and slung the other about her slim shaking figure. 'Little lady, it isn't like you to let go like this—come on, snap out of it.'

'Easy for you, Wade,' she said chokingly. 'You thrive on danger and don't care about anything else, but those savages use knives as well, and I—and I——'

'Here, you stop that!' He drew her against his shoulder and pressed his hard cheek down against her hair, rocking her a little, like an infant in his cradling arm. 'I'd smell them as well, don't you realise that? They aren't so fond of bathing as you and I, and there's nothing so penetrating as acrid human sweat. I'm a soldier, honey. I'm trained like the damned tiger to whiff the air, and there was nothing in the bush that wore pants. Only a hungry trotter——'

'Oh, Wade!' Eve flung her arms about his neck and buried her face in his warm skin. 'Y—you'll be glad to be rid of me, won't you? You'll say goodbye with a great sigh of relief.'

'Sure, I'll be relieved when I get you on that plane to London Airport. I made that promise to myself when you had to be parted from the nuns—little lady, haven't I told you before, we're just two people who got mixed up in a revolt and got thrown together for a while. It's like that film, with Bogart and Bergman, we have to say goodbye because that's how the script is written, honey. But don't think I won't miss you—the way you look in the mornings, all ruffled up and warm, like a kid almost, wanting salt and water to brush your teeth, and being so good about eating dried fish instead of scrambled egg and bacon. Drinking that coffee brew of mine as if it were the best Brazilian blend. Believe me, honey, if my Larry ever finds himself a girl like you, then I'll——'

'Don't!' Her arms hugged him fiercely. 'Don't talk to me as if I'm a schoolgirl waiting to grow up. If I wasn't grown up properly before I met you, I am now, and it hurts, Wade. It hurts!'

Later, lying with her back to him on the blanket, upper body netted, and her legs wrapped in the plaid robe, Eve let the tears roll silently down her face, heavy and salty across her lips ... her lips that hungered and must be denied.

Would the hurting get any easier once she was back in England? Would his features and the sound of his voice gradually fade from her memory? This was how the script was written, he had said, but this time he was the married one, and she must fly away from him knowing that he must stay tied to a woman he didn't love.

Eve was sure of that ... it was her only consolation.

All that night she dozed fitfully and kept starting awake, brought out of her sleep just after dawn by the persistent throbbing in her hand. She sat up carefully and took a look at Wade ... he lay on his back, the Breda by his right hand, his lashes shadowing his cheeks as he slept, so that very briefly he looked vulnerable. Eve studied him for a long moment ... this was the last time she would awake in the morning to find Wade beside her. The man she had slept with, the tough mercenary soldier, who had treated her with a gallantry she would remember and cherish all her life.

'I love you,' she whispered. 'I love you, Wade O'Mara, with every scrap of my heart and every bit of my body.'

Then, taking care not to disturb him, she drew herself out of her cocoon and taking her dried towel made her way to the river, using it to flip away the big webs that were so heavy with dew that the spiders had vacated them.

A mist lay over the water and over the sun, and everything seemed remote and mysterious. As Eve knelt to wash her face she saw a harmless pepper-and-salt snake glide out from a dark-green bush and slip across the big tree roots. On the far side of the river she could glimpse the brown *hadidas* flapping on the water, and soon they would be joined by water-fowl and spotted deer and even a tawny lion or two, who this early in the day only wanted to drink cool water before the pink sky turned into a hot golden one.

Eve examined her left hand and caught her lip hard between her teeth when she touched the yellowish sore spot. It had festered, and Wade would be angry with her if she showed it to him like this. Taking a corner of her towel, she dipped it in the water and bathed her thumb, flinching as she squeezed out the gathering, feeling a dew of sweat break out on her face.

She wouldn't tell him, for he had enough on his mind. Today they began the last lap of their journey and she knew he would be anxious to get to Tanga before nightfall, in order to get her off his hands, and to report to his senior officer. They'd have held Tanga from the insurgents if possible, and she couldn't selfishly pray that a whole town had fallen just to make it possible for her to remain with the man she loved.

As she walked back to their camp site a speckled dragonfly danced ahead of her on huge gauzy wings, a glorious thing, like a flying jewel. And when she paused a moment to collect her composure, she saw, utterly still on a twig, a praying-mantis like a small green ghoul, waiting on its victim with a patience as terrible as its awful little face. The dragonfly and the mantis seemed to typify for Eve what she had found in the jungle ... unexpected moments of beauty ... nerve-wrenching moments of suspense.

Wade had shaved and was pouring coffee when she joined him. He flicked his eyes over her face as he handed her the steaming mug. 'You didn't sleep too well, did you?' he said. 'I felt you tossing and even heard you muttering when you did drift off to sleep. Worrying about the situation at Tanga?'

She nodded and sipped the coffee, whose sweet smokiness made it palatable. They both knew what was really troubling her, but today they must keep everything impersonal.

'I'll dish up the fish,' he said.

'Not for me, thanks.' Eve couldn't have eaten a bite, for even the hot coffee couldn't dispel that sickish feeling at the pit of her stomach. 'I'm not hungry——'

'You should eat something, for once we get on the river I'm going to keep at it and we shan't be camping again today.'

'I—I can eat something in the boat later on.' She handed him the mug so he could pour his own coffee. 'Don't force me, Wade. I just haven't any appetite at present.'

He nodded, but was frowning to himself as he ate his own piece of fish and washed it down with the last of the brew. They packed everything and loaded the canoe, and Eve settled on to the seat, pulling down over her eyes the coolie hat he had made for her from plaited straw and leaves; it was rough and ready, but it shaded her eyes and the lining of leaves kept her head cool. Today it also had the advantage of partly concealing her eyes, which being the servants of her emotions kept straying to Wade as he wielded the paddle. His much-washed shirt was in a faded, torn state by now, and as the sun grew more fierce the khaki began to darken with moisture and his black hair clung in damp strands on his forehead.

Today he wouldn't offer to let her paddle for a while, nor would she ask, for her left hand was hurting badly and the pain seemed to be in her wrist as well. She could feel the pressure of heat like a weight on her shoulders, and it must have been around noon when her head began to feel light, and the occasional sound of Wade's voice seemed to be across the river instead of a few feet across the boat. Her throat was dry as a bone and when she reached for the water-bottle it slipped out of her grasp and she fumbled about in a listless way before retrieving it. Her lips shook against the rim when she tilted it to swallow the cooled boiled water, and dry as her throat was, the rest of her body felt sticky with perspiration. Her heart thudded and a feeling of acute dismay swept over her ... oh God, she couldn't be feverish, could she? Not today, when Wade had made up his mind to reach Tanga and be rid of the responsibility of her.

She had to hold on and not be any more of a burden to him than she had been.

'You okay, Eve?' he asked, and again his voice seemed hollow and far away.

She nodded. 'I—I'll have a little nap to make up for last night.' She slid down into a small heap, feeling as if her bones were dissolving.

'You do that, honey,' she heard him say. 'When you wake up, we'll be home and dry.'

Those were the last words Eve was conscious of, for when her heavy eyelids sank down over her eyes she fell into the depths of a fever from which she awoke a long time later ... home and dry, indeed ... in the cool, ivory-walled bedroom of her guardian's house in Essex, where she had slept as a child and during the school holidays.

She awoke thinking she was home from school; her face was hollowed and her foxfire hair was cut close to her head and the red gleam of it was dimmed.

Eve had no recollection of Major Wade O'Mara, and was not to have any for a long time to come ... jungle fever, trauma, exhaustion, had taken their toll, and she lay languidly in her fourposter bed at Lakeside and believed herself to be recovering from a schoolgirl illness. The nurse who came and went in the lovely, high-ceilinged room didn't make any attempt to put her wise ... that she had been like this for five weeks, ever since they had carried her off the last plane from Tanga, before the town had been overrun by the rebel army.

CHAPTER EIGHT

EVE leapt to meet the ball with her racket, swinging a graceful, slicing stroke that sent the ball whizzing past her opponent's shoulder. He laughed even as he lost the game to her, and ran towards the tennis net that divided them, the sun agleam on his rumpled dark hair and alight in his grey eyes. A very attractive young man in his white shirt and slacks, who gazed across at Eve with an appreciative smile as she spun her racket in the air and caught it, clad herself in a white tennis dress that revealed her slim tanned legs.

'Come up to the house, Larry,' she invited, 'and have some tea with me.'

'With pleasure!'

He joined her outside the hard court and they strolled together across the lawn towards Lakeside, considered one of the most gracious houses in this part of Essex. At the rear of the rambling, mullioned, red-tiled house was a lake and a gazebo, and sunken gardens aflame with wall-roses at this time of the year.

Midsummer, and one of the warmest England had enjoyed for many a year, so that tennis was frequent and there was usually a friend or two for Eve to play with.

They entered the lounge through open glass doors, a long cool room whose walls were silver-grey, the perfect background for the fine suite of Regency furniture and the few fine paintings. Eve watched as Larry Mitchell looked around him, an appreciative gleam in his eyes ... Eve liked his eyes, and whenever she looked into them she felt a vague stirring of recollection, as though he reminded her of someone she had seen and forgotten.

'You live in a nice house,' he told her. 'It suits you, Eve, to have gracious surroundings, and yet at the same time I suspect you have a streak of wildness in you somewhere—it comes out when you play against a chap, or ride that creamy-coated mare of yours. You seem to have two sides to you.'

'Hasn't everyone?' She pressed a finger to a bell attached to the wall. 'We've all a sunny side and a shadowy one, haven't we? You as a budding doctor should know about the complexes and traumas that make people what they are. Are you still enjoying it at St Saviour's, training under Clavering? It was he who operated on my arm that time I nearly lost it.'

Larry winced when Eve said that, and half-shyly he reached out and took hold of her slim left arm, running his fingers down to the inner part of the thumb where all that was left of that intricate operation was a white scar.

'It's hard to believe, Eve, the way you can slam a tennis ball across the net, that you ever had blood-poisoning so bad that you almost lost your arm—such nice arms!'

'Are you flirting with me?' She smiled a little, and found him very attractive and easy to tease. Larry never lost his temper, and yet she suspected that he, too, had a certain amount of temperament in his make-up. He had very definite views about certain things and once or twice had fallen into arguments with her guardian about the way the country was being run.

'Rebellion is hard to put down once it flares,' he had

148

said the other evening. 'It could happen in England just as it's happened elsewhere.'

'Nonsense.' Charles Derrington had lit a fat cigar and puffed smoke with that self-confident air of his, as if, Eve thought, Victoria was still on the throne and England was still a mighty empire with nothing to fear from anyone. 'With all our faults, Mr Mitchell, we're a civilised nation of people and could never commit the atrocities on each other that these—er—foreigners are committing.'

'What about Belfast?' Larry had asked, and Eve had seen a very grim look come to his face when he mentioned that strife-torn city.

'The Irish are hot-headed,' her guardian had replied. 'Always have been, always will be.'

'I've a bit of Irish in me,' Larry had said, and Eve smiled to herself as she recalled the look which her guardian had directed at the tall, dark-haired trainee doctor, whose eyes of light grey were so darkly fringed. Since Charles had given in reluctantly to her insistence that she wouldn't be forced into marriage with James, he seemed to regard every young man who came to Lakeside as her prospective bridegroom. He had very nearly lost her to illness eighteen months ago and since then he had been far less demanding and autocratic. She was all he had, for Charles Derrington had never felt the urge to marry, and they had been closer to each other since those days and nights of restless fever and pain, culminating in a fearsomely poisoned arm which she had very nearly lost.

She felt Larry moving his thumb against her skin, and very gently but firmly she drew away from him. She liked him and was glad they had met at the St Saviour's dance, where she worked as a nursing aide, but she wasn't in love with him ... not yet, at least. Somehow Eve felt no inclination to fall in love, she merely wanted to be of use and to enjoy her leisure hours with genial companions.

A capped and aproned maid wheeled in a trolley, with a silver teapot and bone china tea-service laid out on a lace cloth. Everything in Charles Derrington's house was run in a very gracious and conventional manner; in Eve's eyes the old dear was hopelessly old-fashioned and one of the few people these days who was able to command absolute old-world loyalty from those he employed.

'That looks lovely, Hilda,' she said to the maid. There were thinly sliced cucumber sandwiches, fruit scones and strawberry tarts. 'Thank you.'

The maid gave a bob and withdrew, and Larry stood there shaking his head in amazement. 'I feel each time I come to Lakeside as if I'm transported back into the Thirties. I believe that's when your guardian decided to stop the clock.'

'It's possible.' Eve gave a laugh and gestured to him to take a seat. 'And do help yourself to sandwiches.'

Larry sat down in a deep armchair and watched Eve as she poured the tea, adding the cream and sugar they both liked. The sun through the long windows found red lights in her hair, which was a careless cascade on her shoulders, a foxfire contrast to her smooth honey skin. When she handed him his cup he looked into her eyes, a deep topaz, lovely and seemingly untroubled.

'Are you Irish on your father's side?' she asked, leaning back with her own cup of tea, and feeling very much at ease in his company.

'No, my mother's.' He sipped his tea appreciatively. 'She came from County Mayo and still has a brogue,

150

and some of their special sort of charm with a dash of the devil mixed in. I suspect I have some of that in me, for I enjoy locking horns with your guardian.'

Eve gave a chuckle. 'He's mellowed with age, believe me. There was a time when he might have thrown you out on your ear for daring to oppose his conservative ideas. But I believe he rather likes you, Larry.'

'Do you like me?' Larry's eyes grew beguiling in his lean face. 'I've never met a girl like you, Eve. It isn't only that you're lovely, but you have a kind of gallantry about you—you don't have to work at the hospital doing and seeing things that aren't very pleasant, yet you do it cheerfully and even seem to get a kick out of it. I believe there's a core of steel inside that sweet cool body of yours.'

'Just listen to the blarney,' she mocked. 'I work because it would drive me mad with boredom to sit about the house, arrange the roses and go to card-parties in the afternoons. I need the stimulation of a job, and I once made myself useful at a mission run by nuns.'

'That was out in Africa, wasn't it?' He bit into a sandwich and regarded her slim, charming figure with amazed eyes, as if she seemed too young to have packed into her life that kind of experience, from which she had returned a very sick person, even yet unable to recall all the details of her escape from Tanga.

'Yes—Africa.' Eve frowned and felt again that elusive memory that seemed always to be fretting the edge of her outward content. 'I was with the nuns and somehow we got away—someone got us away.'

'It must have been frightening for you—Eve, what made you go out there in the first place, knowing there was trouble brewing?'

'A man,' she laughed. 'I didn't want to marry him, so

I ran away—it's like something out of a true-hearts serial, isn't it?'

'You mean you were expected to marry him regardless of your feelings—a girl like you?' Larry's eyes held a sudden blaze. 'You'd have to love and be loved —madly.'

'Love?' She nibbled a scone. 'I think love is a barrel of honey and broken glass.'

'How uncomfortable you make it sound!' Larry gave her a curious look, slightly laced with jealousy. 'Are you speaking from experience?'

Eve stared beyond the windows towards the trees, for at this end of the lounge they looked on to the lake and there the tall green and gold willows were thick ... almost jungle-thick. 'I don't know,' she said. 'I have some odd mental blanks left from that time I was ill, and then I ask myself if it's possible for love to be forgotten if we've ever experienced it. What do you think?'

'If love had been painful for you, then you might want to forget it,' he replied.

'Yes,' she nodded. 'Perhaps the man didn't love me in return, but all the same it's provoking not to remember. Don't we shut from our minds our unbearable sins and our equally unbearable sacrifices?'

'Sensitive people might.' Larry leaned forward and searched her face with his grey eyes, and Eve found herself staring into those eyes and feeling again that odd, elusive flicker of remembrance. 'I think you're one of the most sensitive girls I've ever met, and possibly one of the most passionate—curiously enough those two go hand in hand.'

'Passion and sensitivity?' she murmured.

'The ability to feel a high degree of emotion either

way,' he said. 'The trouble is I can't imagine what kind of man could let you go if he knew you cared for him. He'd have to be—ruthless.'

'Ruthless,' she echoed, and then she gave a slight, almost cynical smile. 'I think love is a small harbour on the borderland of dreamland, and that's all I'm doing, I'm dreaming there was something when there was nothing. Have a strawberry tart. They're home-made and delicious.'

'Thanks,' he took one and bit into it. 'Are you happy, Eve?'

She considered his question, slim legs curled beneath her on the couch. 'I think I must be, Larry. I have a nice home, a guardian who no longer treats me as if I were an Edwardian box of candy to be handed to the most suitable suitor, and I'm interested in my hospital work. I think I'm reasonably content with my life. What about you, Larry?'

'I'm doing the work I've always wanted to do, and I've had the good luck to meet you, Eve. You often invite me to Lakeside and I'm wondering if one day you'll come and meet my people? They live in London, near Regent's Gate, and they'd be terribly pleased to meet you. I could drive you up in that little bus of mine, if you'll agree to come.'

Eve considered his invitation and was just slightly worried by it. She didn't want Larry to get serious about her, yet on the other hand it would seem unkind if she refused to meet his family.

'Do say you'll come,' he coaxed. 'I have a free afternoon next Sunday and if the weather stays like this it will make a nice run into London, and my little bus isn't too bad. I was lucky to get it—had a rather generous birthday cheque all the way from Morocco.'

'Morocco?' Eve looked intrigued. 'Have you a relative out there?'

He nodded and his eyes filled with an eagerness that was boyish. 'It's my mother's cousin. He's been quite a rover in his time, and now he's settled down to produce citrus fruits on this rather tumbledown estate he took over about nine months ago. He seems to be making it work, which doesn't surprise me, for he's that sort of man. Hard in some ways, but you could trust him with your life. I—I can't help admitting I'm fond of him, apart from which he helped with my education —sent money so that my people could let me train to be a doctor. My dad is a train driver, you see. He loves the work, but no one pretends they earn a fortune, so the money always came in handy.'

'I think I like the sound of your family, Larry.' Eve had suddenly made up her mind. 'I'd love to meet your parents—I've always been fascinated by train drivers.'

He grinned, a long line slashing itself in his left cheek, making her stare at him and think how attractive he was—youthful-looking, of course, but in a few years' time he'd be quite a man.

'I'll pick you up about noon next Sunday and we'll go to lunch with Ma and Pa, if you'd like that. Roast beef, batter pudding and baked potatoes—you can't do Dad out of his Sunday traditional.'

'Sounds lovely,' she said warmly, and leaning forward on impulse she pressed Larry's hand with hers, moving back adroitly when he would have caught her fingers to his lips. Eve shook her head at him. 'Friends don't get soppy, and I want us to be friends—for now.'

'Leaving me with a little margin for hope?' he quizzed her.

154

'You're young, Larry, and the world is full of girls. Some of those nurses at St Saviour's are very attractive in their uniforms, especially in that blue cape with the little chain across the throat.'

'None of them can touch you,' he rejoined, running his eyes over her hair and face. 'You have something extra—a little air of mystery, I think.'

Eve laughed and went to the piano, where she sat down and began to play a dated but still tuneful melody of a romantic era lost down the pages of time ... *I'll see you again, whenever spring breaks through again* ... Eve didn't know why it haunted her, but somehow it did. Then with a careless laugh she broke into a more modern tune and said over her shoulder to Larry:

'If you're off duty this evening we could go and dance at the Beach Club. At least the band plays civilised, schmaltzy music.'

'I'd like that.' He was standing right behind her and she tensed. 'Play that other tune again—that more sentimental one. It's a Noël Coward song, isn't it?'

'Yes, and hopelessly sentimental.'

'Rather lovely, I thought. You often play it, don't you? Is it a favourite of your guardian's?'

'Good lord, no!' Eve laughed at the mere idea. 'Charles is an ardent fan of Leonard Bernstein and he deplores my fondness for the light stuff, as he calls it. Charles likes a full orchestra playing something very deep and complicated—he considers my taste in music, books and drama very flighty considering what he spent on my education. Dear Charles, he really should have had a daughter of his own who might have taken after him, as it is he's landed with me.'

'He's a lucky man,' Larry murmured, and though she had warned him not to kiss her, he suddenly leaned down and brushed his lips across the top of her head. 'I wish I could take you dancing, Eve, but I've got to get back and sign in for some emergency duty, and you know what Saturday night can be like when the football crowds are in town. But it is definite about next Sunday, isn't it? It's a firm promise?'

She turned round on the piano bench to look at him, seeing a lock of dark hair across his forehead and something in his face that made her study him before she replied, unaware that a little sadness shaded her mouth for a moment.

'Yes, a firm promise,' she said. 'Have you got to go now?'

He glanced at his wristwatch and nodded, twisting his mouth and giving her a wistful look. 'You're a temptress, Eve, but duty calls and I've just twenty minutes to make it to the hospital. Noon on Sunday, and it won't come quick enough for me!'

'Nor me,' she smiled, and saw him to the front steps, where his small low-slung car was waiting for him. He swung in behind the wheel and she waved him goodbye, watching until the yellow car swung out of the gates on to the main road. It was quiet after Larry had left and Eve began to stroll in the direction of the garden, where the bright roses were entangled in rays of sunlight, and where the leaves scarcely stirred in the warmth of the afternoon. Suddenly she felt faintly depressed and the scent of the roses seemed to add to her feeling of ... now what kind of a feeling was it? She paused and put out a hand to touch a rose, which broke and scattered its petals the moment her fingers came in contact with its velvety loveliness.

She watched the petals drift to the path ... love might be like that, she thought. One moment a glowing thing in the sunshine, and the next a sad little heap of memories.

Loss ... yes, that was what she felt. Could it be that saying goodbye to Larry had induced this feeling in her? Was she growing fonder of him than she had realised, or thought wise? He was very genuine, good company and most attractive in a lean dark way, but he was younger than she, not only by a year, but in other ways ... emotional ways.

She wandered on towards the lake, cool and shimmering and faintly dyed with red as the sun began to decline in the sky above the willows. She leaned against a tree and rubbed the forefinger of her left hand against the scar down the side of her thumb.

She wished it would all come back to her, what had happened to her in Africa, but all she knew from her guardian, and it seemed he had got his information from the flight crew of the plane on which she had travelled home to England, was that a rough-looking soldier had carried her through the gunfire and the burning streets of Tanga and after seeing her safely aboard the aircraft had vanished into the raging noise and confusion of a town under siege. He had safety-pinned a note on Eve's shirt telling the crew her name and where she lived, but beyond this they knew nothing of the man, and Eve often wished she could have found a way to thank him. When she had tried to contact Sister Mercy and the other nuns she had received the shattering reply that they had been killed when a shell had landed on the mission where they had been working in Tanga ... Eve had wept when she received such sad news about those kind, brave, self-sacrificing women.

Why, Eve wondered, her gaze on the darkening lake,

did kindness and goodness have to be so cruelly rewarded? Or was it true that the pure in soul found their haven high up there beyond all the clouds, all the sorrows? She hoped so, and further hoped that somewhere that rough-looking soldier was still alive and hadn't perished in the fighting at Tanga.

Peace was now restored there under the new President, and Eve hoped it would last and the wild loveliness of Africa could flourish again and the wonderful birds and beasts return to their old haunts, to fish and hunt and stretch tawny in the sun.

Oh lord, she was getting hopelessly nostalgic and had better return to the house before those silly tears started up again. She had no reason to cry . . . her guardian was good to her, and on Sunday she was driving to London with Larry to meet new people and exchange fresh ideas. Life was good, and she thrust away from her that strange shadow that sometimes seemed to haunt her . . . a memory that wouldn't take shape much as she tried to clothe it, to give it shape and form and words.

She shrugged and entered the house, to breathe cigar smoke and hear the sound of masculine voices in the study, where the door was partially open. She peered in and there was Charles with a couple of his business friends, and she was about to withdraw when he noticed her.

'Eve, there you are, child. Been playing tennis, eh? Come along in and meet Stephen Carlisle, who is over here from New York to buy up all the best paintings at Christie's. And you know Tyler, of course.'

'Hullo, Tyler,' she smiled at one of his guardian's oldest friends, and held out her hand to the tall American, who had one of those ugly-attractive faces in the

Abraham Lincoln tradition. As he shook hands with her, his brown eyes ran over her slim, white-clad figure and her hair that had a foxfire gleam under the lights of the study.

'When I say it's a pleasure to meet you, Miss Derrington, I mean it.'

'Thank you,' she said, wriggling her fingers which he held on to. 'But I'm the ward of the house, not the daughter, and my surname is Tarrant.'

'I see.' He smiled, showing big strong American teeth. 'Is that Miss Tarrant?'

'It is.' She cast an appealing glance at Charles. 'Do tell your friend that I'd like my hand back so I can go and change for dinner.'

But her guardian chuckled and looked rather pleased with himself as he drew on his cigar. Ah, thought Eve, so the American was wealthy and Charles was matchmaking again. Well, that wouldn't do, for Eve had already decided that if she was going to let love into her life, then she couldn't do better than let her friendship with Larry Mitchell grow into something warmer and closer. There was something about Larry ... the more she saw of him the more he appealed to her. She wished of course that he was older, but they had plenty of time to develop their relationship, and with him she'd be a companion rather than a possession.

Stephen Carlisle looked the type who would regard a woman as he regarded the paintings he bought, something to be owned and admired, but whose opinions would be disregarded. Eve made a determined effort and pulled free of his handclasp. She saw his thick eyebrows pull together and she knew she was right about him ... he was the arrogant, rather humourless type who thought his money made him irresistible.

'I must excuse myself right after dinner,' she told Charles. 'I have a date at the Beach Club.'

'Surely you can break it?' he said, giving her a slight frown. 'If it's with young Larry Mitchell, then he'll forgive you.'

'You underestimate Larry,' she replied, uncaring that she had told a white lie in order to escape the further attentions of Stephen Carlisle; she'd drive to the club, for there was always someone there whom she knew and could dance with. 'Larry is very strong-willed Charles. He's taking me to meet his parents on Sunday.'

Her guardian clamped his teeth on his cigar and Eve could see that he was none too pleased by her piece of information. She knew he quite liked Larry, but for him there was no denying that the young student doctor was poor and struggling and hardly the auspicious match that he wanted for his ward. She saw the struggle he was having with his temper, and then he shrugged his shoulders.

'You're a sensible wench,' he said. 'You'll do the right thing in the end, and I'm not saying that young Mitchell isn't a rather handsome lad, but he's far too young for you, Eve, and you know it. I know you, girl, don't think I don't. You like older men—always have.'

'Dear Guardy,' she laughed, 'to hear you speak you'd think I was always chasing the local grandfathers! Larry's a dear——'

'He's a cub, and you'll ring the Beach Club and tell him you can't make it tonight because I need you to play hostess to my guests.'

'Is that a direct order?' she asked, standing there in the open frame of the door, her chin tilted and her eyes defiant. She hadn't needed to defy him in a long time, and that alone told her that he was banking on Carlisle making an impression on her. Good lord, was he a millionaire?

'Yes,' Charles gave a curt inclination of his head, 'you may take it as an order, Eve.'

'All right.' Tonight she wouldn't argue with him. 'But I shan't be letting him down on Sunday. I'm going to lunch with his people—it's something I want to do very much.'

With those words she left the three men and walked across the hall to the curving staircase, feeling the heat in her cheeks as she ran upstairs and hurried along to her suite. No, she wouldn't let it start all over again, that coercion into a marriage she didn't want. Life with James would have been vapid and monotonous, but there was something about Carlisle's mouth that warned her he was a sensualist as well as an art collector. She actually shivered when she thought of that thick mouth with its full quota of hard white teeth descending on hers ... it reminded her ... Oh God, she raked her fingers through her hair and tried to pull the tormenting memory out of her reluctant mind. Something terrible, frightening, which must have happened to her out in Africa. Had someone attacked her ... had the soldier who had put her on the plane saved her from that attack?

Eve took a shower and all the time she was dressing her mind was probing for an answer to that question. It was awful to have a gap in her memory and to feel that it was important that gap be filled in.

The mirror gave back her reflection to her, outwardly poised and composed in a tulle dress in palest

161

green, with eyelet embroidery in the full sleeves. She sprayed on perfume and stared at the container. *Tabu* —now why had she bought that the last time she had called in at the pharmacy in town? She usually bought *Je Reviens*, which was slightly more discreet.

She met her own eyes in the mirror as she fastened a string of pearls, glossy as satin against her throat and a get-well present from Charles just after she recovered from her illness and came home to Lakeside from the hospital. She smoothed her hair, which fell in a glossy auburn wave down over her left profile ... Garbo, she grinned, about to sit among the men and look like a *femme fatale*. She must remember to tell Larry about that season of Bogart films they were putting on at the Classic cinema ...

Eve caught her breath, for suddenly, like a jab, she almost seemed to remember something ... someone imitating that inimitable star of the golden era of Hollywood.

'Here's looking at you, kid.'

Eve raised her hands to her cheeks and her eyes begged ... begged for the memory to complete itself. 'Who are you?' she whispered, glancing around her bedroom. 'Why do you haunt me like this? What were you to me ... please, please don't hide from me!'

But all she saw was a lovely, high-ceilinged room furnished with a Queen Anne bed, slipper chairs upholstered in gold with hints of green, a handsome rosewood bookcase that curved at the sides, and an array of long windows draped in brocade reaching to a carpet woven with flowers in ivory against leaf-green.

A graceful, sedate room, where only two men had ever entered, her guardian and her doctor. The ghost that flirted with her memory had nothing whatever to do with this room, this house, or any part of Lakeside and its surrounding country.

It was someone she had known out in Africa, and as her hand slid down her face, her neck, finding her heart, Eve knew that he was dead. Yes, she knew the feeling now; it was an ache, a deep sense of very personal loss, which meant that she had cared for him. Who had he been ... what had he been, that unremembered man for whom, unaware, she wore *Tabu*?

She went downstairs and sat composedly at dinner with the three men, listening politely to their conversation, and ignoring the compliments that lay in Carlisle's eyes each time he looked at her. They had fresh local lobsters stuffed with onions, mushrooms, breadcrumbs and grated cheese, baked to a golden brown; steamed chicken with melon and shrimp, followed by iced coffee-cream. Her guardian had once served in a Government post out in Barbados, and he was still fond of the food and had it served at Lakeside at least twice a week.

'A most excellent meal, good sir.' Carlisle leaned back in his chair and looked as sleek and replete as a well-fed wolf, Eve told herself. 'If you and Tyler are going to smoke, may I ask Miss Tarrant to invite me for a stroll on your lakeside terrace?'

'By all means, Stephen.' Charles ignored Eve's glance of appeal. 'A cigar is the solace of the middle-aged man, but you're entitled to enjoy the company of a pretty girl. I believe there's a midsummer moon, and our lake is a picture you won't be able to buy with your dollars. Run along, Eve, show our American friend what an English garden can look like in the moonlight.'

Eve wanted to run, but even before she reached the door Stephen Carlisle had his hand beneath her elbow, his fingers closing upon her arm so that she'd look undignified if she tried to shake free of him. 'You won't need a wrap, will you?' he murmured. 'The night is warm and I'd hate you to cover up that charming dress.'

Eve knew what he really meant, that he didn't want her to cover up the slim figure which the dress flattered. 'I really would like my cloak,' she said in a cool voice. 'Although the midsummer days are warm, the nights are quite chilly.'

'You sound rather chilly yourself.' He held her under the hall lights and forced her to look at him. 'Don't you like me—Eve? Women usually do.'

'How nice for your ego, Mr Carlisle,' she rejoined. 'But I happen to have a rather nice young man who works very hard for his living, and it would be unfair to him if I allowed other men to get the idea that I'm —free.'

'Your guardian has assured me that nothing of a definite nature exists between you and this young man, and even so, Eve, I wouldn't be put off by even a fiancé if I felt strongly enough attracted to a girl, and you're very attractive.' His eyes slid over her. 'It really is true, isn't it, that English girls have an outward air of coolness, even aloofness, but they smoulder beneath it. I came to England not only to buy works of art for my house in Manhattan, but I came in search of a wife——'

'Mr Carlisle,' Eve pulled forcibly away from him, 'I am not in the marriage market, no matter what my guardian might have implied. I am not up for auction like some—some damned painting! I live my own life and I choose who I want to care for, and you are not the type of man I could ever imagine myself caring for!'

'How your eyes take fire when you get aroused,' he drawled. 'Funnily enough, I like you better for not falling into my arms right away, for when a man is rich there are too many women ready to throw themselves at his head. You really intrigue me, Eve. You really make it sound as if you prefer some impecunious medical student to a man of considerable means—what are you, honey, some kind of a romantic?'

'Perhaps I am.' She tossed her hair and it gleamed with deep tawny lights. 'I expect we're a dying breed in this age of meretricious love affairs.'

'More and more do I like you.' A smile curled around his heavy mouth. 'Little did I realise when I accepted an invitation to Derrington's house that I'd find a gem of a girl in his collection of rare stones and coins, which was my direct reason for coming here. Now aren't you going to show me the lake from the terrace?'

'I'll fetch my cloak.' Eve walked across to the big oak closet in the hall which contained odd coats and wraps. The cloak she wanted was an old black velvet one with a cowl, and as she took it from the closet she could feel Stephen Carlisle staring at her and moving his gaze up and down the silken fall of hair over her left eye. She swung the cloak around her and quickly covered her hair with the cowl, and she saw his teeth show hard and white against his tanned skin as he studied her.

'Are you hoping that outfit makes you look like a nun?' he enquired.

Eve disdained to answer him and moved across to the small flight of curving stairs that led to the terrace. She opened the glass doors and stepped out into the night, moving to the curved parapet, built like this long ago to accommodate the wide crinolines of the era in which Lakeside had been erected.

She stood tensely by the balustrade, aware of Carlisle's tall figure behind her. Above them was the milky radiance of the midsummer sky at night, with a glittering shell of a moon reflected in the still water of the lake. The reeds in the shallows were softly rustling and the willow leaves were whispering ... it was a glorious night and Eve could feel that ache in her heart that Larry Mitchell was possibly too young to assuage, and this man Carlisle too self-centred to ever understand.

'Your guardian is right about his lake,' he murmured. 'It really is a picture that would be hard to put upon canvas with any justice. Tell me, Eve, has he never wanted to have your portrait painted?'

'When I was eighteen,' she said, 'but I didn't like the idea. Portraits should only be painted after people have really lived—and suffered.'

'So that they have character, eh, and don't resemble birthday cards.' He stepped round to her side and leaned an elbow on the parapet, the moonlight on the angular planes of his face. 'This is how I would have you painted, Eve, clad only in this cloak with the cowl thrown back on the nape of your neck, your eyes upon that glimmering lake as if you see there what other people haven't eyes to see. What is it, I wonder? The golden sword of some knight in shining armour?'

'What nonsense!' she scoffed, even as her fingers clenched the stone balustrade. 'I'm not that foolishly romantic, Mr Carlisle.'

'Won't you call me Stephen?'

'What would be the point?' she asked coolly. 'I shan't be seeing you again after tonight.'

'From any other girl I would construe that remark as a hook doing a little fishing.' He leaned nearer to her. 'I very much want to see you again and I shall let your guardian know this quite frankly. He knows your worth, Eve. He won't allow you to throw yourself away on a medical student who even when qualified will earn barely enough to support a wife—least of all a young woman who has been accustomed to the kind of life Charles Derrington has provided for you here at Lakeside. Could you really live in a cramped apartment, making ends meet on a few pounds a week? Could your romantic feelings survive on that kind of love?'

'I imagine real love could survive any kind of odds,' she rejoined. 'If I married Larry I'd go on working so that we could pool our earnings. I'd be his partner, not his possessions.'

'My dear Eve, you were made to be a man's possession,' he laughed, softly and sensuously. 'Come, be honest with yourself. You know in your heart that you don't want a boy but a real man, one who has had experience of life, who can show you the world, and bring out all the glowing woman in you. There is such a woman in you, coolly restrained at the moment, held in chains that need to be broken by a strong man. Then what a change in you, running madly to him with your hair like a vixen's in the sun.'

Eve stared at him and felt a sudden throb of the heart. Why did his words strike her as familiar ... a vixen in the sun he had called her, but it wasn't the first time a man had said that to her.

'That is the colour of your hair, isn't it?' he drawled. 'Vixen red?'

'I—I suppose it is. If you've seen enough of the lake, shall we——'

'No.' His hand closed over hers, tightening those big, well-manicured fingers about hers. 'I like your company, Eve, and I don't want to lose it. Allow me to book seats for the theatre, and afterwards we could go on to a supper club. Allow yourself to get to know me. Some of the greatest love affairs have evolved from antagonism at first.'

'You're very sure of yourself, aren't you?' Eve exclaimed. 'I've only ever known one other man who——' There she broke off, glancing away from him towards the lake. She listened to those mysterious night-time sounds that the water made as it rippled around the reeds and moved the willow tresses. She stared at the water and she did seem to imagine that someone might come moonlit out of the lake, shaking the drops off black hair, tough and primitive as some animal of the jungle. Eve shivered, for his ghost was walking again, but when she peered forward across the balustrade there were only trees at the edge of the lake and nothing tangible for her to reach for.

As she sighed, Carlisle's fingers tightened painfully on her hand.

'Who was this man you speak of? He was important to you, eh?'

'I think he was——'

'Where is he now? Do you still see him?'

'You——' Eve turned her head to look at the American, a stranger to her until tonight. 'You have no right to question me about him. You have no hold on me, so don't go assuming one!'

'No hold, you say, eh?' Abruptly he pulled her to him and was bringing his lips down to crush hers when she swiftly turned her head and his mouth descended on the velvet cowl and she heard him curse.

'Let me go Mr Carlisle, or I shall let loose a scream and tell my guardian that you tried to rape me—our rape laws in England are still rather grim especially if the ward of a local magistrate should be involved.'

His arms fell away from her and he forced a smile to his face even though his brows were meshed together above thwarted eyes. 'You've quite a sharp little tongue on you haven't you, Eve? You're overdue for a bit of taming that's your trouble. Is that how you lost the first man and why you're now running around with a bit of a boy? Does it frighten you when a man exerts his strength?'

'Any bully can show his muscles,' she said scornfully. 'When a woman wants to be kissed she enjoys that superior show of strength——'

'You mean you've actually enjoyed being kissed?' he sneered.

Eve didn't even bother to reply to him but walked away down the steps to the hall and across to the drawing-room where she looked in to say goodnight to Tyler and to wonder as she wished her guardian goodnight how he could thrust her on to someone like Carlisle and assume that she'd be dazzled by his money and ignore his arrogance with regard to women.

'Where's Stephen?' Charles enquired and a little hard glint came into his eyes such as she remembered from the days when she had fought not to be thrown into marriage with James. Oh God she thought tiredly how mistaken you could be about those who were supposed to love you, or at least care what became of you.

169

'Gone to the devil for all I care,' she said, and there was a chill little note of disillusion in her voice. 'And you might as well know, Guardy, that he won't be putting in a bid for me—he's found out that I don't go for the branding-iron type of charm. I'm my own person, Charles. I earn my own living and I stay under your roof because I thought you wanted my company, but if we're back to the old system of selecting a rich man to keep me in heart-rotting idleness, then I pack my bag and leave in the morning. Goodnight!'

Eve went upstairs, feeling unhappy and nervy. She clung to the thought of Larry ... he at least wanted her for herself, with none of this bartering her body and soul for the sake of a socially acceptable and financially suitable match, regardless of whether it made her happy or miserable.

Inside her bedroom, with the door firmly closed, she lay stretched along the length of her bed, her face buried deep in her arms. She didn't weep but felt waves of grief and hopeless longing sweep over her. She wanted love ... the love she had lost somewhere on the other side of the earth ... somewhere on the other side of heaven. It was an active pain deep inside her and she knew ... knew with every fibre of her body and heart that she loved the man and she was never going to see him again. And he had cared about her ... cared as no one else ever had, and her fingers clenched the bed-cover and she felt as if never again would there be anyone in her life who would love her so selflessly.

'What was your name?' she whispered. 'Why can't I remember your name or the way you looked when I remember with my heart that you loved me?'

She sat up, staring into the wash of moonlight

through the windows where the drapes were open to let in the air. Her heart was beating fast and she was seeing the flames of a burning town, hearing the gunfire, feeling the hard clasp of arms as she was carried through the streets to the airfield. A rough-looking soldier, they had said, who placed her in the care of the stewardess and then vanished back into the flames and the fighting.

A soldier, torn, grubby, unshaven, making sure she got to safety, and then turning back to face the bedlam ... and to be killed.

He was dead, otherwise he'd have come to her, found her again, put those hard arms around her and made her safe for always. The hot tears filled her eyes, and she was crying her heart out when Charles Derrington came into her room and switched on the light.

'Good heavens, child!' He drew her against his shoulder and stroked her tousled hair. 'Are you feeling ill?'

She fought with the tears and shook her head.

'Then why are you upsetting yourself like this, talking about packing your bag and leaving me? Tyler gave me a ticking-off, d'you know that? Said I was pushing you again and you aren't a girl to be pushed on to any man—look, what is it, my pet? Do you want to marry that young doctor, is that it? Think I won't approve? Well, if that's what you want. Eve, then maybe we can see about making him some kind of an allowance so that he can—well, I don't want you living in rooms somewhere, going hungry, or anything like that——'

'Guardy,' she drew away from him, her face tear-streaked and the tip of her nose pink from weeping, 'I —I don't want to marry anyone—not yet—maybe not

171

ever. Don't you understand? There was someone—someone I loved so much that it still goes on hurting a—and I don't—can't put anyone in his place. He loved me and saved my life,' the hot aching tears fell again from her eyes and burned against her lips. 'He's dead and I can't stop my heart from aching for him, a—and the awful part is that I can't remember the very last thing he said to me—the very last time he kissed me. I just know he loved me and I—I want him—I want him, Guardy, and he's dead!'

She was weeping unrestrainedly now, trembling and grieving for what she had lost. Charles soothed her as best he could, but now she had given way to the pent-up emotion she couldn't seem to restrain it.

'Why couldn't I die with him?' she sobbed. 'Why must I go on alone?'

'Who was this man, Eve?' Her guardian made her look at him through her wet, unhappy eyes. 'Why haven't you mentioned him before?'

'I—I think my mind found parting from him so unbearable that it didn't want to remember, but now I know—it was the soldier who put me on the last plane out of Tanga, that awful day when the insurgents took over and the fighting was so bad. He made sure I was safe, that I'd be brought to England, and then he joined in the fighting a—and got himself killed.'

'My dear child, how can you be so sure he was killed? What was his name? We can check with the War Office——'

'He was a mercenary and I—I can't recall his name. I only knew we were madly in love with each other——'

'That rough-looking soldier?' Charles looked at her askance.

'Wouldn't you look rough, Guardy, if you were fighting your way through the smoke and blood of an uprising?' Eve made a determined effort to pull herself together, wiping her face with the handkerchief Charles gave her and taking a couple of deep breaths to calm herself. 'I know in my heart he was the most gallant man I ever met... I shall never know another like him.'

'Eve, you're young and you mustn't talk like this— there's every likelihood that if the fellow isn't dead and you saw him again, in ordinary circumstances, you'd realise that the glamour and danger of being rescued by him made him seem like—like some bold knight who snatched you to safety. War has that effect on people. It heightens all the emotions and a meeting that in normal circumstances would seem fairly mundane takes on dimensions out of the ordinary.'

'No,' Eve shook her head and in her heart was very certain of what she had felt for her unknown soldier. 'He was very special to me, Guardy, and that's why I'm so impatient with men like Stephen Carlisle. He's so full of his self-importance, and if danger ever threatened him, he'd stamp all over those who got in his way to the safety exit. Guardy, would you really thrust me on to a man like that?'

'It seems you wouldn't let me.' Charles gave her a quizzical smile and stroked the hair from her brow. 'You've a mind of your own, and it seems, a heart. What about young Larry Mitchell? You are aware that he's fond of you?'

'I like Larry enormously, but I'm not thinking in terms of marriage, Guardy. It will take him several years to become fully qualified, but in the meantime I enjoy his company, and I've agreed to meet his parents. I'm looking forward to Sunday.'

'They're Londoners?'

Eve nodded. 'They live near Regent's Gate, though his mother came originally from County Mayo. They sound very nice.'

'Then you go and enjoy yourself.' Charles pressed his lips to her forehead. 'And I'll promise not to invite Carlisle to Lakeside any more. A pity he's not your type, my pet. Seems he has enormous holdings in land and property——'

'Oh, Guardy!' Eve had to laugh. 'You'll always harbour the Edwardian idea that marriage is made in a bank and not in heaven. My dear, marriage means living with a man in a way more totally personal than any other kind of living, and I couldn't give myself if I didn't respect and admire beyond all others the man I married. Call me hopelessly romantic if you like, but that's the way I'm made. Love means more to me than money ever could—I believe I could live in a mud hut on real love.'

Charles, who loved his cigars and his comfortable home, gave Eve a perplexed look. 'That's easily said, my child, but if you ever tried it you'd soon change your tune.'

'But I have tried it,' she heard herself say, but she spoke so softly that Charles didn't really catch what she said, and was rising to his feet with a yawn.

'Get a good night's rest,' he said. 'You'll feel more yourself in the morning—it's only at night when the ghosts walk, eh?'

Eve nodded, and when he had gone she lay for some time on her bed, visualising a future that would never hold again the love she had found in Africa. It was lost, but very gradually the memories were coming back to her and one day soon she would remember everything ... she would see again in her heart the face she had loved.

Hear again that beloved voice ...'Here's looking at you, kid ...'

CHAPTER NINE

THE car radio was playing as they drove along the London Road, and the soft warm wind was blowing Eve's hair and bringing colour to her cheeks. Acker Bilk playing as only he could the plaintive *It Had To Be You*, lovely nostalgic words and a deep rich melody, softening her lips to poignancy.

'I bless the day for keeping fine,' Larry said. 'We had a shower last night and I feared it was going to break up the weather.'

'Nature's tears,' Eve murmured, 'clearing the air. What a day! That breeze is like silk.'

'That's what I like about a soft-top car,' Larry enthused. 'I hate being closed in, don't you?'

'It's smothering,' she agreed. 'Ah, *Greensleeves*! Don't you love it?'

'I think I may love you,' he replied, shooting a glance at her. She wore a sleeveless dress the colour of palest dahlias, with an embroidered cluster of small dahlias on the left hip. Her scent was by Guerlain, and her legs looked elegant in sheer nylon, her feet clasped in slender strapped shoes. She had known that he wanted her to look her best and had complied to the last detail, but the smile she gave him was just a little anxious.

'Love is a big word, Larry, and we've all the time in the world to get around to it. Don't let's be serious. Let us enjoy what we have right now.'

'I'll do anything you say,' he smiled, 'but I just wanted you to know that no matter what you did, no matter if you had to hurt me, I'd still feel a very special love for you. Even if I could never have you, you'd always haunt me—that's how it is, sometimes.'

'Yes,' she murmured, 'I feel that too.'

They arrived at Regent's Gate just before one o'clock, and Larry's mother must have been watching for the car from the front room window, for she was at the door and it was opened before Larry could even touch the bell.

They embraced silently and Eve saw the happy tears glisten in the deep blue Irish eyes ... funny, but she had expected Larry to have his mother's eyes and decided that he must take after his father.

'Ma, this is Eve.' Larry drew her forward, a slight flush in his cheeks and a lock of dark hair falling across his brow. He introduced her with such obvious pride that Eve wasn't surprised when Mrs Mitchell gave her that considering, rather reticent look of the fond mother who suddenly realises that her son has become a man and has developed an eager interest in a young woman.

'How do you do, Mrs Mitchell.' Eve held out her hand and when Larry's mother shook it, Eve noticed that she gave that hand a surprised look, as if she had expected the smooth pampered skin and nails of someone who was decorative but slightly useless.

Eve smiled. 'Hasn't Larry told you that I work at the same hospital as he does? I'm a nursing aide.'

'Larry told me you lived in a lovely big house in Essex,' Mrs Mitchell explained, as they made their way across a small hallway to a pleasant lounge furnished in oak, with blue velvet curtains drawn back from the bay windows. 'I expect our house must seem very small to you, Miss Tarrant.'

'It's charming,' Eve said sincerely. 'I see you have a

piano. Do you play, Mrs Mitchell?'

'No, but my husband's fond of a tune. Please sit down.' She gestured at the blue velvet sofa and Eve felt the quick up-and-down look that Larry's mother gave her as she sat down and crossed her slim legs. Eve wondered if her dress and perfume were a little too sophisticated, but how could she explain that she hadn't come to lunch as a prospective daughter-in-law but as a friend of Larry's? Mrs Mitchell was obviously thinking of her in terms of imminent relationship, and Eve just had to reassure her.

'It's nice for Larry to come to Lakeside; he's able to use our hard court and to keep fit for all that studying and hard work he has to do. You must be very proud of him, Mrs Mitchell. There's so much more to being a doctor these days, and it's relaxing for him at my guardian's house. He and Charles often play snooker together, has he told you? They get along fine—in fact we're all very good friends.'

Eve emphasised that word and held on to the deep blue gaze of this nice woman of modest means who was obviously afraid that her son was mixing with moneyed people who might turn his head. 'You have nothing to worry about,' Eve longed to say to her. 'Larry has a good firm head on his shoulders and he'll thoroughly enjoy making his own way in life because he's basically tough and tenacious.'

Eve glanced at him and wondered a little why she felt so sure about his character. What was it about him that made her so certain he had that inner core of strength that would always be his standby, so that he'd enjoy challenge and accept adversity? He looked so young with his dark ruffled hair, sitting there on the

178

piano stool, long-legged and relaxed.

'Where's Dad?' he asked. 'He's not had to go on duty, has he? I wanted Eve to meet him.'

'No.' Mrs Mitchell broke into a smile that banished the anxiety from her face. 'He's gone out for a drink with—you'll never guess, Larry!'

'The Minister of Transport,' Larry said, with a grin. 'Pa would love to get him into a corner with a few of his ideas on how to improve our transport system.'

'Someone, my dear, who flew into London yesterday with sand on his shoes!'

'You're kidding!' Larry exclaimed.

His mother shook her head and her eyes were sparkling. 'It was a lovely surprise, opening the door to him and seeing him so fit and dark as an Arab. And he's had such good news from the lawyer!'

Larry smiled and turned to look at Eve. 'My mother's talking about her cousin—the one I told you about who has a citrus farm on the edge of the desert. His arrival will really make it a party—I take it, Ma, he's staying to lunch with us?'

'You couldn't stop him,' she laughed. 'He wouldn't miss tucking into my roast beef and pudding. Oh, but it is good news for him, after all these months of uncertainty—the lawyer has now confirmed absolutely that he's free of that woman he married. It seems that about ten years ago she went out to Las Vegas to work as a croupier, where she obtained an American divorce and remarried. About three years after that, when she must have been in her middle thirties, she had one of those operations to restore the figure and it seems that only a few hours afterwards she collapsed with an embolism and died. It was the change of name that stumped the

179

lawyer, but now everything is confirmed and that broth of a man decided he'd earned a spree in London.'

Mrs Mitchell put her hands to her flushed cheeks. 'You must forgive me for gabbling on like this, Miss Tarrant, but we're all very fond of my cousin, and because he lost touch with his wife years ago he could never be certain—well, you know how it is. He's a man in his prime and now he's settled on this fruit farm he may want to chance a second marriage. The first was a total disaster—he married a woman who was incapable of loyalty, trust or love. He didn't deserve that, not my cousin.'

'Doesn't she go on about him!' Larry grinned. 'That's family loyalty for you.'

'It is indeed.' Eve smiled at Mrs Mitchell. 'Won't you call me Eve? I'd very much like you to.'

Mrs Mitchell's slight look of constraint reappeared, as if once again she visualised Eve as a daughter-in-law who would gradually involve Larry in a life-style more sophisticated than the one he had always been accustomed to.

'Would you like a cup of tea—Eve? Or perhaps a coffee?' she asked.

'I'd very much enjoy a cup of tea,' Eve replied. 'Coffee's inclined to give me heartburn.'

'Not too often, I hope?' Larry gave her a concerned look, the future doctor overshadowing his look of youth.

'No,' she laughed, 'but I will eat those canteen doughnuts with it, and then more often than not I have to dash round with the tea trolley and so, doctor dear, I get indigestion.'

'Whereabouts exactly?' He leaned forward with a serious air. 'You show me where you get the pain.'

'It isn't a pain, you idiot,' she said. 'Like everyone

else these days I don't relax enough, and when I feel peckish I fill up on the crispy things that I burn off again by dashing about in the wards. I'm perfectly fit, Larry.'

'But nervy,' he said. 'Sort of strung up. You need a holiday.'

'Where would you suggest?' she smiled.

'Morocco?' murmured a voice near the door.

Eve sat very still and in the silence that followed she could feel her heart beginning to thud, and then Larry had leapt to his feet and was loping across the room. 'Wade!' he exclaimed. "How great to see you, and Ma was right about the tan! What do you do, laze about in that desert sunshine all day long?'

'Some hopes of that! Let me look at you, Larry—you're keeping spare, and you've a tan yourself.'

By then Eve had found the courage to turn and look ... to find a ghost or a living man. The voice had done it, turned the key that unlocked all the memories, every single one of them, and slowly she stood up and her eyes clung to that lean, dark, inimitable face. Wade O'Mara ... the cousin of Moira Mitchell, whom Larry called mother.

'Hullo,' Wade said softly. 'And how are you, dear deb?'

'Don't——' Her voice shook wildly. 'Don't call me that, Major.'

'What would you like me to call you?' He was walking towards her and there was no one else in the world, and the walls of this London house were falling around her and she could smell the jungle again and hear the birds and the rush of the river, cascading down from the brown cliffs.

'Eve!' His hands had hold of hers and the lost dream

had become a living reality again; strong tough hands, brown as teak, clasping hers as if this time he'd never let them go again. 'Lovely tempting Eve—did you guess, did you feel it, that I'd find you again, some time, somewhere? Did you long for me as much as I longed for you?'

His eyes, like steel all alive and glowing in his darkly tanned face, ran over her hair, her face, her figure in the sleeveless dress. 'So this is how you look, my jungle waif, when you aren't slogging through the bush in outsize sandals and a torn green shirt—yet I love that picture of you, and I've carried it in my heart for a long time—too long a time.'

'What is this?' Larry demanded. 'Do you two know each other?'

'I think we do,' Wade smiled, his eyes still feasting on Eve's face, which from sudden paleness had gone to a wild, joy-stung rose. 'We met in the jungle, and you'd never think to look at this fragrant, charming young woman that I've seen her as scratched-limbed and tangle-haired as some wild girl of the woods. What a pair we were, Eve! Did you ever dream we'd make it?'

'Wade,' the luxury of his name was like wine in her mouth, 'oh, Wade, why did you stay away from me so long?'

'Because it took time, my dear love, finding out if I had the freedom and the right to come and claim you. When young Larry wrote to say he'd met a girl called Eve Tarrant, it came hard not to write back to say I knew you as well—knew you better than anyone else on earth.'

Wade turned to his son—his son who had no idea

that this tall, lean, grey-eyed man was his father, though the likeness now they stood together was striking. 'I love this lady,' Wade said simply. 'And a lovely lady she is—I couldn't offer her less than marriage, and for years I'd not seen or heard anything of my wife and I didn't know if she was alive or dead. It took time finding out, and now——'

He paused significantly and his hands tightened possessively on Eve's.

Larry drew his underlip between his teeth, his grey eyes staring a moment into his father's. Then he looked at Eve and she knew what he saw ... he saw the love she couldn't hide or deny or ever lose again ... her love for Wade.

'So this was the guy who got you out of Africa?' Larry said. 'It's a small world.'

For Eve it was suddenly a wonderful world, and she could feel herself smiling at Wade with the funny and the tragic memories all mirrored in her eyes. How well he looked! How vital and sure and ready to make a life for them together. She swayed a little with the happy reaction of it, and he caught her to him and when his arms closed around her she gave a sigh of pure satisfaction and knew she was safe in that harbour on the edge of dreamland.

'You're pleased to see me, then?' he murmured.

'Delirious.' Her eyes smiled up into his, lustrous with love. 'Will I wake up to find you gone again?'

'Not in this life,' he promised. 'Do you reckon young Larry will forgive me for taking his girl away from him?'

They both glanced at Larry, who had his hands thrust deep into his trouser pockets and was regarding them with a frown ... a studious, intrigued frown.

'Do you know,' he said, 'I never realised before that people in love have a look of being part of each other. It's fascinating. You two really do belong together, don't you?'

'Some boy, isn't he?' Wade said quietly, with more meaning than his son could ever realise. 'You'll go far, my—my young cousin.'

Larry shrugged, grinned. 'I could punch your nose in, Wade, except that you'd probably punch my head in! She's a great gal—you take care of her.'

'I intend to.' Wade locked his arm securely about Eve. 'I won't let go of her any more—the last time hurt too damned much.'

At that moment Mrs Mitchell walked into the lounge with the tea-tray, and a thin, humorous-faced man with sandy hair followed her. 'Guess what, Dad,' Larry said to him, 'these two know each other! Would you credit it? I bring a girl home for the first time and this darned mercenary comes strolling in and takes her away from me.'

'That's a mercenary all over,' Stan Mitchell smiled, strolling to the tall young man who called him father. He flung an arm about the slim shoulders and hugged Larry. 'You've plenty of time for love affairs, my boy. You've got to work hard and become a fine doctor. That's what we'd like to see, eh, Wade?'

Eve saw the glance that passed between the two men and she knew that Larry would never be told that the tall, lean mercenary Major had fathered him. Later on she learned herself from Moira Mitchell that while Wade had been stationed with the regular army in Malaya his wife had badly neglected the baby boy, and upon Wade's return to England he had flung her out of his life, acquired custody of his son and placed him in the care of his cousin and her husband. It had seemed easier, better for the child to be called Mitchell and to think of the couple as his parents. The years had gone by, until the moment had slipped away for telling him the truth. Wade didn't want him to know the truth, that his mother had been a tramp who had cared more for a good time than her husband and child.

Larry loved and respected the Mitchells, and they in their turn had grown to think of him as their very own son. Wade would do nothing to alter that ... the complex pattern of fate that brought love and pain and wasn't to be struggled against. It had its way with everyone, for good or bad, and watching Wade at the lunch table, looking the same and yet looking so attractive in his well-cut grey suit with a speckless white shirt and dark grey tie, Eve felt a surge of happiness so close to tears that she had to bite hard on her lip in order to hold them back.

She reached out instead and touched his hand as if to make sure of his reality, and she saw Larry glance at them as Wade carried her hand to his lips and kissed it.

Eve met Larry's eyes and silently begged him to understand that it hadn't been her wish to hurt him. but the love she felt for Wade was so strong, so irresistible, so hungry after all the waiting, the hopeless build-up of feeling that he must be dead because he didn't attempt to find her again.

But he had been hoping for his freedom ... searching for it with the help of a lawyer, and when it came into his grasp he had been unable to stay away from her any longer. She smiled into his eyes, this man who had

185

saved her life more than once, and who had now saved her heart from being closed to a glowing, joyful love ... the love she had thought lost somewhere in Africa.

After lunch she and Wade slipped away into the garden, there to kiss and to talk of the future ... their future together on his fruit farm on the edge of the desert.

'You'll love the smell of citrus and desert winds,' he said. 'At dawn, and at the fall of dusk. I've recently bought a pair of Arab horses and we'll ride, Eve—we'll take long gallops across the sands and enjoy all that sense of freedom together.'

'It will be heavenly—oh, Wade, I thought I'd never see you again, never hear your voice, never see this deep line in your cheek when you smile at me.' She reached up and drew her fingers down his warm dark face. 'You sent me away from you—you told me to go and marry a man of my own age. What made you come to your senses? What made you realise that our kind of love couldn't be torn out of the heart as easily as that?'

'Riding alone in the desert,' he murmured. 'Wanting you there beside me with the desert sun shining on your foxfire hair, and needing you in my arms when the moon shone across those sands and turned them to silver and sable. God, how I wanted you! When Larry wrote to me about you, I was staggered—he's my boy and I was tempted to be noble and let him have you. But you're mine, Eve!' His arms tightened possessively around her. 'I brought you through the jungle and saw you safe aboard that plane—mine, my own darling deb, with spirit and courage and so much warmth of heart. You belonged to me—to me, and I was lonely as hell. I had to come and get you. I figured that Larry's only a boy and with him it's only calf-love, but with me, it means my very life. I want you! I must have you!'

'You have me, Major.' Held close and hard to him beneath an apple tree, she smiled, then suddenly reached up and plucked an apple. 'May I tempt you with this, darling?'

'I don't need an apple to be tempted by you, lady.' And tilting back her head he laid his lips on hers in a kiss whose piercing sweetness and desire she would remember all her life. The apple fell to the grass as she curved her arms about his neck and held him close to her ... for always.

A WORD ABOUT THE AUTHOR

Violet Winspear, who says she began "scribbling" at the age of three, is one of Harlequin's busiest authors. Her first Romance, *Lucifer's Angel* (#593), was published in 1961. Her first Presents, *Devil in a Silver Room* (#5), appeared in 1973. She is a member of the select group of authors who have produced more than fifty Harlequins.

Violet's father, who died when she was very young, left her a love of books as a legacy. While still a schoolgirl, she adored inventing stories, and at the age of fourteen she began work at a book bindery. When she turned to writing romances, the author spent more than a year on her first manuscript, working at it in her spare time and sharing her secret with only her mother.

With pride this Harlequin author will tell you that she is a true Cockney, born within the sound of London's Bow Bells. And although she now makes her home at a seaside bungalow, she likes to return to her old haunts in the city's East End and remember the people she knew.

These old friends have walked through the pages of her books in many guises. "And," Violet Winspear confides, "they would have laughed and been slightly embarrassed had I told them they would inhabit Spanish capitals and tropical islands, and marry into the aristocracy!"

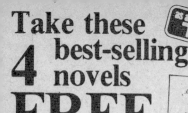